THE HURRICANE

BY HUGH HOWEY

The Hurricane

Copyright © 2011 by Hugh Howey

ISBN-13: 978-1-461-05944-8
ISBN-10: 1-461-05944-5

www.hughhowey.com

Give feedback on the book at:
hughhowey@hotmail.com

Printed in the U.S.A.

For Paul

1

It was the last day of summer, and Daniel Stillman spent it looking for a girl. He grabbed his mouse and scrolled through the list, paying as much attention to the number of viewers listed by each window as he did the small picture inside. He had learned to shy away from the girls with hoards of onlookers, but also to avoid those with just one or two voyeurs. While Daniel was loathe to compete with a crowd, he was also reticent of those who couldn't draw one. Screen names went by: jasMine21, dancegurlz, StacYnKate. Daniel clicked on one, adding the chat window and webcam to the cascade of other potential dates for the evening.

While the loading advertisement rolled, he checked his appearance in his own webcam window. Daniel had on a pair of ripped jeans, his feet tucked up underneath him, the rips clearly visible on video. Excellent. For his t-shirt, he'd picked out a fake vintage Pepsi, the blue of which showed up nicely on screen. Part of the press-on logo was melted from a botched job of ironing the shirt, but he thought the extra damage was a nice touch. It looked more than a few months old.

The only flaw he could see was that his hair wasn't perfectly messy. He licked his palms and ran them up the sides of his head while Ford wrapped up their attempt to sell him a car he could never afford. He ran his fingers through his short choppy hair one more time, his coordination stymied by the correct-facing video, which undid seventeen years' experience of combing his reflection in a mirror. He finally gave up and made one last adjustment to the webcam. It brought a heap of dirty laundry into the screen behind him, which forced him to move the cam back rather than get up and deal with it.

Finally, leXie213's video stream popped up, revealing a window into a teenager's bedroom. Lexie, he could only presume, was bent forward, pecking at her keys, her head distorted from being so close to her camera. When she leaned back, Daniel could see that she was lovely. And laughing. He glanced down her chuckling neck, past her loose tank top, and at the chat window beneath her image, scanning for the origin of her mirth:

LuckyLuke: show us your tits!
leXie213: I was thinking Amherst, but am applying to State n case.
DwistfulPoet: Amherst would be nice.
roBBerBaron: she ain't gonna show em.
DwistfulPoet: What major?
LuckyLuke: unstrap them puppies!!
leXie213: Marine Biology
roBBerBaron: c'mon, just a quick peak..
DwistfulPoet: Kewl. U into fish?
leXie213: yup
LuckyLuke: then free them guppies swimmin in yo tank!!

Lexie was still laughing. She rested back on a low wall of pillows on her bed. The lower half of two unrecognizable posters could be seen hanging just above the headboard. Daniel figured both were vampire-related by the red font on almost solid black backgrounds. As Lexie leaned forward to rattle off a reply, he stopped sizing up her room and focused on the aforementioned breasts. Was she really laughing at this Luke character? And was "tank" a reference to her tank top? If so, how did these guys come up with shit like that so fast? And how could a girl like Lexie laugh at someone screaming to see her tits?

Daniel sized up his competition. They were arranged in two rows of little cubes off to the right of Lexie's much larger chat window. None of her other suitors displayed the barest hint of over eagerness and desperation that Daniel felt. They looked relaxed. Half of them wore large trucker hats with bills pressed sheet-metal flat. Somehow, they were able to not look ridiculous in them.

Daniel knew he would have. He'd tried them on.

Not a one of the boys smiled, even as Lexie laughed. They wore the frozen expressions of the serially dis-interested. One boy glanced in his coffee cup, swirling it around. Another held a guitar on his lap, his shirt off, looking like he wasn't even aware he was on camera. They each exuded a calm and confidence that Daniel recognized as intoxicating to the opposite sex, some-thing as impossible and awkward to arrange in himself as it was to sort out his hair with the webcam. Their chiseled jaws made his comparatively thin face look more like the chisel. Two of the kids had rounded shoulders like water balloons. With shoulders like that, Daniel could imagine asking to see a girl's tits and being laughed at in a *good* way.

He grabbed his Winamp window and placed the squiggly lines of a Coldplay tune over the double row of trucker studs. Daniel's confidence was shaken. He imagined his webcam window arranged alongside the others and wondered what Lexie would think of the boy who looked different from the rest. And not different in a cool, hipsterish way. Which was to say: the same.

When he looked back to Lexie, Daniel saw that she had taken a call. She laughed into her cell phone, and he wondered if she was maybe talking to one of the dozen other guys peeking into her life. Daniel quickly typed that she had a gorgeous laugh and watched as his message scooted up the screen, chased away by catcalls, talk of college, and pleadings for more tits. Lexie's eyes never made it back to her computer before his little flirtation was gone. This beautiful girl, sitting in any one of hundreds of millions of upstairs bedrooms all across the globe, laughed and rolled her eyes at something said on the other line. She ran a thumb under one of her tank top straps and adjusted it, caring little for what innocent gestures did to less innocent onlookers. Coldplay quit their wailing and Winamp moved randomly to a song by Train, the squiggles dancing madly over the sort of guys Lexie was more likely into.

Daniel adjusted his webcam and thought back to the beginning of the summer and the one time a girl in a video chat had given him her number to call. It had turned out to be a prank, or something more like a marketing scam. The video of the girl had been a loop, not a live view at all, and his traced call had started a flood of text ads for 1-900 sex lines and links to websites with names like: sexyhotblondes.ru.

Two hours of wrangling with AT&T customer service had eventually netted him a new cell phone number, which put an end to the embarrassing flood. A stolen minute with his mom's and stepdad's cell phones, a quick edit of his own entry in each, and they weren't the wiser. It wasn't as if either of them knew his number by heart. Hardly anyone knew anyone's numbers anymore.

His sister and brother had to be told, as parting either from their phones for even a minute would've required more patience than Daniel possessed. His excuse for the change of numbers was that he had someone stalking him. They both seemed to know it was something worse (and more likely) as they updated his contact info.

The only other person Daniel had to tell was his best friend, who was away at a steady stream of camps all summer and couldn't have called if he'd wanted to. Daniel thought about how little difference there'd be in the density of incoming calls now that nobody else knew his new number. The porn spam, if nothing else, had made him feel popular for a few weeks.

Train quit their whining, and *A Puddle of Sunshine* lit into a ballad of pathetic crooning. Without the temporary silence in between, Daniel probably wouldn't even know his playlist was ticking through the songs. It was one long emo-ish rant of false badassery. Still, any one of the lead singers could probably log onto the webcam site and have a gaggle of fawning beauties *begging* to show their tits. Daniel considered that as he commented on the color of Lexie's eyes, hoping that would somehow lead her to remove her tank top in a way that outright demands seemingly weren't. The kid with "poet" in his name called Daniel a faggot, which seemed doubly unfair. Lexie laughed, and Daniel couldn't tell if it was at his comment, the insult, or the myriad calls for "more skin" that shoved his false innocence off the top of the screen.

He didn't ask.

Instead, he flicked his cam off and closed the half-dozen chat windows, most of them already dark from rejection. Summer was coming to a close—and Daniel was unzipping his pants.

He shrugged the machine-ripped denim down to his knees, yanked two tissues from the Kleenex box, and pulled up Youtube. A quick search of "booty shaking dance underwear," a promise that he was, indeed, one year older than his birth certificate actually suggested, and Daniel was presented with a veritable army of virus-free soft porn that could not reject him.

And so Daniel Stillman's summer concluded much as it began, interrupted only once and for a brief pause as someone thundered up the carpeted steps, rushed past his bedroom and violently slammed their door, leaving Daniel to flacidly wonder, only for a moment, if he'd bothered locking his—

2

Breakfast the following morning was a return to riotous familial clamor as everyone in the house found themselves squeezed into the same routine once more. After months of getting out of bed to find his mom and stepdad already off to work, his sister stalking the mall an hour before it opened, and his brother still in bed and snoring, Daniel was reminded why he hated school year mornings. It was the jarring sense of crowded loneliness in the packed kitchen. Everyone got in everyone else's way. Daniel fished a clean bowl out of the open dishwasher and plucked a spoon from the bottom rack before sorting through the open boxes of cereal haphazardly arranged across the counter.

"And here's our little senior," his mother said. She clacked over on her heels, her pinstriped business suit bringing a whiff of noxiously familiar perfume. She gave Daniel an awkward, one-armed hug from behind while sipping loudly on her coffee—right in his ear.

He started to say something about how little he was looking forward to his senior year, but she was already gone, pressing the plastic lid onto her wide-bottomed travel mug as she click-clocked, click-clocked out of the kitchen. The jingling of her car keys and the ding of the burglar alarm as she opened the front door were familiar goodbyes.

The kitchen immediately felt more crowded, and Daniel felt more alone. He dug his spoon under his cornflakes as he drug a chair away from the small dining room table with his foot. Carlton, his stepdad of two whole years, looked up from his iPad at the squeal of the chair on the tile.

"Sorry," Daniel muttered around a full mouth.

He watched his sister, Zola, text furiously as he shoveled his breakfast down. Her thumbs were like feet on a duck, paddling madly while the rest of her hovered serenely above. Daniel was often startled by the texts he received from her. Paragraphs of jargon-heavy code popped up one after the other while he fumbled to reply to the first thing she'd said. Attempts to actually call her were futile. His sister's phone was used to do everything except take actual calls. It hadn't taken long before Daniel had given up on communicating with her. Most of what he knew about his sister he now discovered second and third hand through Facebook. His classmates would ask him about some guy she was dating, as if he knew.

Daniel's older brother, Hunter, sat at the head of the table, opposite his stepdad. A half-eaten breakfast burrito sat in front of him on the silvery box in which it had been microwaved. Hunter frowned and bit his lip at the PSP cluctched tightly in his hands. He steered the device left and right, his face twitching with effort. By the sound of the heavy metal tunes blaring from his brother's earbuds, Daniel pegged it as the latest Need for Speed racing game. He had given the game a spin a week ago, but Hunter had gone ballistic when he'd wrecked some car his brother had spent two weeks upgrading and modding to perfection. It looked like a fun game, but Daniel wasn't likely to get a chance with it again anytime soon.

So the four of them sat in a buzzing, clackety, spoon-chiming silence while Carlton finished whatever morning news blog he was reading on his iPad. When he shut the thing off and slid it into its black padded portfolio, it was a sign for the rest of them to scatter for their book bags, to hastily brush their teeth, to try on a different t-shirt, and all the compressed chaos that made the formerly relaxed calm of the morning transform into the suddenly hurried.

"Let's go, let's go," Carlton sang by the front door.

The burglar alarm chimed. Dishes crashed into the sink. Hunter ran by with a cold burrito; Zola skittered along, her thumbs dancing; Daniel rushed after them both, his shirt on backwards. They exited into the too-bright morning sunshine and piled into Carlton's Volkswagen. Well-engineered doors slammed tight with a muted patter. As Carlton backed out of the driveway, heading off first toward the community college to drop off Hunter, and then to the high school to unload him and his sister, Daniel gazed out at the hazy blue of his South Carolina sky. The sleepy coastal town of Beaufort slid by, waking up as the sun beat down. Daniel could feel its heat on his face as the rays were trapped between him and the side window. In the distance, a line of thick clouds sat low on the horizon, hunkered down and quietly brooding. Daniel paid them little attention as the lines of zooming cars, all in a rush, sped by in the other direction.

3

Daniel had waited his entire life to be a senior in high school. His brother was two years older, but had been held back in the fourth grade when coping with their parents' divorce had wrecked his long string of Goods and Very Goods. Ever since the humiliation of repeating a grade—and having his younger siblings chase him down a year—Hunter had gone through school distracted and disinterested. He took up smoking earlier than he would admit (but began reeking of it by eighth grade), started hanging out with older kids who had cars, spent enough time in detention to nearly have it count as an elective course, and generally went through life grumbling and playing videogames. What looked like failure, however, made Hunter extraordinarily popular with other kids hoping to get away with doing very little. He and his friends had cast a constant shadow of mean-spiritedness over Daniel that had only been broken by Hunter having (barely) graduated high school. And now, with Zola coming in as a freshman, Daniel finally occupied an enviable position within the family hierarchy. It was the only year a middle child, such as he, would ever have that honor.

Expectations of such magnitude just made his first day as a senior that much more of a colossal disappointment. Daniel's swelling sense of worth and stature lasted from Carlton's Volkswagen to his walk to homeroom. That was when the school principle made the "exciting" announcement that a new digital learning initiative (and a generous grant from Xerox, makers of the most advanced copiers in the world. *Xerox, where copying is good*) would provide every Beaufort High freshman with a brand new Apple laptop.

Cheers could be heard through the painted cinder-block walls of the senior homeroom, obviously from a neighboring freshman class. The collective groan from Daniel and his peers barely dented it.

"We don't get laptops?" Daniel asked nobody.

Mrs. Wingham waved the class down. Everyone else had the same question/complaint.

After homeroom, Daniel bumped into his best friend Roby, whom he hadn't seen since the last day of classes the year before.

"Roby!"

"Daniel."

The impulse was there to embrace after so long a separation, but stigma and mutual social awkwardness intervened.

"How was math camp?"

"Easy as pi," Roby said.

Daniel laughed as dutifully as he figured any best friend should at so obvious a joke.

"Computer camp was better," he added.

"What was the other camp?" Daniel asked with a grin.

Every summer, Roby's parents squirreled away their son in a never ending string of self-betterment camps while they spent their time at various locales abroad.

Roby looked away from Daniel and out over the courtyard. Kids shuffled by with deflated, first-day-of-class backpacks on.

"..."

"I'm sorry," said Daniel. "What camp?"

He knew what camp.

"It was a vocal retreat," Roby whispered.

"Singing camp, right?"

"What did you do with *your* summer?" Roby asked. Daniel listened for any change in his friend's voice, any sign of perfect pitch, but noted none.

Daniel shrugged. "Worked at the carwash. Got in a fistfight with Hunter. Pissed off my sister to no end. Roasted on the beach."

"Did you see that girl again?"

"Nah." Daniel tried to make it sound as if the loss were incidental. *That girl* referred to a fling the previous summer with a tourist from Georgia. Her parents had rented a house on the beach for a week, and Daniel had labored into first base with her, panting and sweating and not even thinking about leading off for second.

"See anyone else?"

"Not really."

"*I* met someone," Roby said.

"No shit?" Daniel felt immediately bad for the way he'd said it. Even worse for the way he looked his friend up and down, disbelieving. The primary reason the two of them were fast friends was because they couldn't keep up with anyone else in the cool department. Daniel's problem (his own self-assessment) was that he was too *normal*. He had tried fitting in with a few cliques: the jocks, the preps, the hipsters, the gamers—but in every case he had felt like he was donning a costume and playing make-believe. His comfortable attire of t-shirt (not vintage), jeans (not skinny), and modern sneakers (not retro) left him looking dull and uninteresting. Anything else he tried just made him feel like a spectacle.

"No shit," Roby said proudly—ignoring Daniel's complete and absolute lack of belief.

Roby's problem (once again, according to Daniel's assessment) was his parents' expectations. He was the smartest kid in school, but mostly because he worked his ass off. He didn't have time for friends, even though everyone knew him. They jockeyed for desks near his, crowded around him in class because he was known as a human cheat sheet. He studied too hard to get anything wrong, and was too overly polite to hide his answers. He wasn't exactly revolting, just awkward and soft of body— but then half the kids in their school were overweight to some degree, and most of *them* still managed to score with the opposite sex.

"You meet her at math camp?" Daniel turned and started walking toward his first class. Roby followed along. "Did she cube your root?"

Roby laughed. "I don't even know what that means."

Neither did Daniel.

"And no, I met her at the vocal retre—at *singing* camp," he said, shrugging his sagging backpack further up his shoulder.

"So she likes sopranos?"

Roby punched Daniel in the arm. "I'm a *tenor*, ass."

"Whatever."

"She and I are kinda steady, actually."

Daniel stopped outside the English building and turned around. He searched his friend for a sign that he might be joking, but came up empty.

"No shit?"

Roby shook his head.

"Where's she live?"

"Columbia."

"How're you gonna see each other?"

A gulf had opened between them. Daniel could suddenly feel it. The earth beneath Beaufort had become a void with just a thin shell on top. One crack, and he'd plummet forever.

"She has a car, so she might come down some weekends. And Mom says she'll take me halfway, up to Orangeburg, to meet her now and then."

"Your *mom* knows about her?"

"We all had lunch together."

"Who?" Daniel heard splintering beneath his feet.

"Me and her and our parents." Roby danced out of the way as a thick plume of jocks burst out of the English building. Daniel tried to move but was assisted by a rough knock against his backpack, sending him twirling.

"You met her *parents?*"

Roby shrugged. The two minute warning bell chimed across campus. "Yeah, and she met mine."

"And everyone's cool?"

"She's Jewish," Roby stated. "Everyone approves."

Daniel looked to the English building, which continued to disgorge stragglers and gobble others in return. He forgot his best friend was Jewish except around certain holidays and whenever he made the mistake of eating over. Now he pictured a wedding and a boy lifted up on a chair, but some of that might've been leftover memories from Roby's Bar Mitzvah.

"So that's that, then."

He said it with sad finality.

"I've gotta get to class," Roby said. He slapped Daniel on the arm. "And you make it sound like I've got cancer or something. You should be happy for me."

"I am," Daniel said.

And I'm miserable for myself, he thought.

"I'll tell you all about her later," Roby called out over his shoulder. He trotted down the sidewalk, his backpack swinging dangerously, a new bounce in his step that Daniel couldn't match up as belonging to his former best friend.

4

Daniel's first glimpse of Hurricane Anna was an aerial view of the storm stolen over Carrie Wilton's shoulder. She had her laptop up at the end of class and had followed a link from Facebook. Daniel was shoving his books and the mountain of "Xeroxed" class handouts into his bag when the twisted white buzzsaw of a storm showed up on her screen.

"Still a category one?" he asked. He'd heard about the storm in his last class.

Carrie glanced over her shoulder at Daniel. "Yeah, and weakening."

"You know it's gonna be a light storm season when we get our first named one so late," he said, trying to initiate some kind of friendly banter. He leaned closer and checked the curved cone of the probability track projected ahead of the storm. Landfall looked most likely for Northern Florida, but stretched into Georgia. It was several days out, which probably meant nothing but rain for the weekend.

"Gonna wreck Jeremy Stevens's party," Carrie said, slapping her laptop shut. She slid it into her purple shoulder bag and squirmed out of her desk.

"Someone's throwing a party *already?*" Daniel frowned. "We just got back. Plus, it's a short week."

Carrie smiled cruelly. "Not invited, huh?"

Daniel adjusted the straps on his backpack, letting the growing weight of all his new books sit higher up his shoulders. "I probably wouldn't go anyway."

Carrie sniffed and twirled away; she joined the shuffling others as his class filed out into the din-filled hallway.

Daniel followed along, the last out of the classroom. He stepped aside in the hallway and fumbled for his schedule, trying to remember where his last class of the day was. Or even what subject it was supposed to be. He pulled a sheet of paper out of his back pocket and tried to read his scribblings from homeroom; his laptop-envious scrawl was nearly illegible.

Around him, everyone else checked their smartphones for their schedules, or were busy texting one another. Daniel watched the flow of traffic for a moment, his brain already numbed from sitting through four classes of teachers droning about what they would be doing in the following weeks. Two girls walked by, both focused on their phones, thumbs flicking in twin blurs. They laughed at the same time, and Daniel wondered if the giggling was coincidence, or if perhaps they were texting *each other* while walking side by side.

A quick scan of the crowd and he saw that he was now officially alone in not having a smartphone. His mother, an insurance adjuster and self-proclaimed addict to her "Crackberry," had resisted even allowing them to get cell phones before highschool. Zola had pitched a fit two Christmas's ago and had gotten a new phone with a slide-out keyboard. Daniel was stuck with a model that could text, but the cramped keypad made it an exercise in futility, especially for someone with slow thumbs like himself. As he watched the surreal, quiet flow of thumb-clacking traffic, Daniel wondered if perhaps his physical unpopularity had something to do with his being a digital non-entity. The summer of the cellphone had arrived, and just in time for him to change his number and downgrade his model (on his own dime). All because of a looped vidchat tease that turned out to be a damned 1-900 trap.

Daniel double-checked the location of his next class, put his notes away, and bent over his basic phone, both thumbs on the keys. He merged with the flow of traffic, jabbing numbers randomly, laughing at nothing, and pretending to be as connected as the rest of his peers: all completely absorbed in what took place between the backs of their hands and on their tiny screens.

****

After his final class—a mind-numbing mathematical affair wherein his teacher crammed three years of review into fifty minutes—Daniel met Roby in the courtyard, where he found his friend absorbed in a game on his new iPhone. It must've been one of the games that used the device's accelerometer, as Roby chewed his lip and cradled the phone in both hands, his elbows thrown wide as he fought to make fine motions with the small screen. Daniel strode up and bumped Roby's elbow, which elicited a sound effect from the game like glass shattering, followed by an explosion.

"You shit!"

Daniel laughed. "What level were you on?"

"Twelve."

"Is that good?"

Roby shoved his phone into his back pocket. "Not really, to be honest. Still, you're a shit."

"Thanks." Daniel tucked his thumbs into his backpack's shoulder straps. "Whatcha feel like doing?"

"I've gotta get home, actually. Jada's Skyping me this afternoon so we can work on this duet we've come up with."

"Jada? That's the girl?"

"She's not *the girl*, she's my girlfriend. And yeah, her name's Jada."

"Is that like Jada the hut? Is she, like, enormous?"

"No, ass, it's from the name Yada. It's Hebrew. It means 'He who knows,' or something like that." Roby jerked his head toward the front of the school where the worn out brakes on the busses could be heard squealing and hissing. He started walking that way, out toward the parking lot. "And she's not fat. She's hot. You'll see."

"Yeah? When?"

"Well, she might be coming down this weekend, actually. I'm thinking of taking her to Jeremy Stevens's party."

"You got invited to that?"

Roby shrugged. "I'm the reason Jeremy didn't have to take summer school. He kinda copied off my finals in English last year."

"And you let him?"

"Yes, I chose to not have my ass kicked after school, and now I'm taking my girlfriend to his party."

"Well, I heard it was gonna get rained out. It was originally supposed to be a pool party or something."

The two boys exited under the bus awning and weaved through a long file of kids in band uniforms, the drummers practicing quietly on their rims, the sax players clicking valves and pretending to blow through the reeds. Each kid seemed to be working on different parts of obviously very different songs.

"The party'll just move inside if it rains. Besides, I hear the storm is dying down and moving more south. It'll probably hit Florida and cross over into the gulf."

"Shit always hits Florida, doesn't it?"

"Yeah. I think God shaped it like a penis on purpose just so he could have fun kicking it repeatedly."

"Haha."

"So, are you going to the party?"

Daniel stopped at the curb. He saw his sister in a cluster of freshman girls a dozen feet away. They were giggling amongst themselves, staring at their phones, a few of them holding theirs up to take pictures or videos of the others.

"I dunno," Daniel said. "It's not really my scene."

"We don't *have* a scene," Roby said. "But you should come. I'd like you to meet Jada. Jeremy will be cool with it."

"Okay. Maybe. Anyway, I'll see you tomorrow if I don't see you online tonight."

"Sounds good," Roby said. He waved before heading through the long file of idling cars and toward the cluster of grumbling buses beyond.

5

Daniel was helping set the tray tables out when his mom pulled up the driveway. It was seven fifteen. He could set his watch to her coming home two hours late, right on the dot. She did it every single evening and always apologized for "being late," even though she couldn't have been more consistently punctual if she'd been German and a train.

Carlton shuffled through the room—his tie off and shirt untucked—and portioned out a *Friday's* frozen skillet sensation-or-something-other onto four plates. Zola staggered around, one thumb texting, the other hand clutching silverware. Once Daniel had the last tray set up, he took the bundle of utensils from his sister and had his usual nightly mental debate over which side the fork and knife went on.

"Fork on the left," Carlton said as he slopped a pile of braised-something and julienned-something-else out of a steaming bag and onto a plate.

Daniel grabbed the remote and started searching through the DVR's list of last-week's shows as the burglar alarm chimed his mother's entrance. The door flew open in the middle of a conversation, his mother explaining to someone else that they were doing something wrong.

Daniel chose "House," his mother's favorite, and fast-forwarded to the opening scene. He paused it there and went to help with drinks while Zola laughed at something on her phone, shaking her head in bemusement.

In the kitchen, his mother's cellphone snapped shut, followed immediately by loud and perfunctory kisses. A purse jangled to a heap on the counter. A jacket was tossed over the back of a chair. Someone complained about their feet, another mentioned a sore back. His mother apologized for being late.

"Are we ready to eat?" she asked. "Wrap that up," she told Zola, suddenly impatient with other people using their phones.

The four of them filed into the living room, and Daniel handed the remote to Carlton, who would writhe as if in pain at anyone else's incompetent attempts to skip commercials in the least optimum way possible.

"House," he said, looking at the frozen image on the screen.

Daniel's mom squinted at the TV. "Is it one we haven't seen?"

"Can I eat in my room?" Zola asked.

"No you can not," their mother said. "Your friends do not want to watch you eat on their webcams while you talk with your mouth full." She jabbed her fork at the TV. "Now sit and enjoy your food while we have some family time."

"Hunter said he had a group project for school, so he's ordering pizza at a classmate's house," Carlton said. He aimed the remote at the TV while their mom swiveled her head around to confirm for herself that her eldest child wasn't in the room.

"Group project? The first week of school?"

"He's in college, now," Carlton reminded her.

"Community," Daniel reminded them both.

His mom shot him a look. The TV lurched into motion, showing a young girl laboring the final hundred yards of a marathon, her face contorted in a mask of discomfort, sweat coming off her in sheets.

"She's not the one," Zola and Daniel said in unison.

They glanced over at each other and smiled.

The camera panned to a cup of proffered water, grabbed at on the run and sloshed on the girl's head. Then the scene cut to a young man in the crowd, clapping and egging her on.

"*He's* the one," their mother said, laughing.

Sure enough, as the ribbon parted across the young woman's chest, her friend in the crowd collapsed, clutching his own. Forks tinked on plates, and the four of them laughed. The spectator crumbled into a heap just as the theme music and opening credits began.

Daniel dove into his food while Carlton worked his magic on the commercials. He didn't need to see the rest of the show, anyway; it would only be slightly less formulaic than the transparent intro. He was more excited to get family time over with and get upstairs to see who was online before passing out for the night.

6

While Daniel and the town of Beaufort slept, two hurricanes gathered steam. One was Anna, the first named storm of the annual hurricane season. She slowly took shape North of the Bahamas, her malformed eye finally winking open, her lungs filling with the powerful warmth of the Gulf Stream.

The other brewing storm was the pervasive digital one sparking at all times through the air. It was the dozens of conflicting weather reports, the several track projections, the weather channels and hurricane centers. The paradox of the digital age was that this plethora of information made it more difficult to hear. With so much available to the consumer, it was easier than ever to tune out *all* of it.

Weather warnings and urgent updates still scrolled along at the bottom of network television shows, but these were recorded on DVRs. They wouldn't be seen until it was too late. Nothing was "live" anymore. Community service warnings had transformed into recorded history, reminding viewers of weather that had already blown through. When a flood warning appeared, it merely explained the previous week's heavy rains.

"Oh, look, that's about the storm we had last week."

"So *that's* why American Idol didn't record the other day. I'm telling you, we've got to switch to cable."

"I wish they'd take these stupid messages off. I can't see the bloody score!"

Car radios still beeped with that awful broadcast from the emergency warning system (only a test, of course), but ears were tuned to iPods, ripped CDs, and satellite radio. The storm brewing off the East coast was literally drowned out by the storm that hung invisible in the air at all times. And amid this virtual sea of information, storms could jog their paths ever so slightly and do so unnoticed. Probability cones might creep, experts might jabber, poncho-packing reporters might cancel hotel reservations and make new ones, but it would be a full day, maybe two, before anyone else noticed. There were more important things to tune into: like Jeremy Stevens's party, who was going, and what to wear.

By Friday afternoon, as projected course cones crept northward and experts explained how a front moving across the Midwest was deflecting Anna more than expected, Daniel was standing by the car pickup area giving into his best friend's demands and agreeing to go to the party.

"So you'll come?" Roby looked doubtful.

"I said I would."

"Do you need a ride? I could see if Jada will stop by and get you."

Daniel waved his friend off. "Don't worry about it. Carlton's taking his car into the shop after he drops us off at home, but Hunter said he'd give me a lift with mom's car. It's on the way to his girlfriend's house."

Roby reached into his pocket and grabbed his phone, which must've been vibrating. He glanced at the screen and started typing a response, somehow able to converse with Daniel at the same time.

"Is your brother still seeing that oriental chick?"

"Her name's Chen. And that's offensive."

Roby glanced up from his text message. "What? *Chick?*"

"Oriental. Rugs are oriental. People are Asian. Think of the continent they live on."

"Whatever. What's racist is naming your Asian child 'Chen.' That's asking for trouble."

Daniel slapped Roby on the back. "My racist Jewish friend. I love it."

"Now *that's* racist."

"Whatever. Hey, my ride's here and your bus isn't gonna wait for you." Daniel waved to his sister and hitched his backpack up. As he walked toward Carlton's car, he heard Roby calling out after him:

"Okay, but I'd better see you there tonight!"

****

Daniel spent the afternoon pacing around the house, waiting on his brother to get ready. Hunter's inability to get anywhere on time meant Daniel was fashionably late to the party, but was sweating and anxious by the time he arrived.

Jeremy Stevens lived on a cul-de-sac, which was already lined two deep with cars when they arrived. Daniel cracked the passenger door of his mother's Taurus, and thuds of bass music rattled from Jeremy's house to compete with the roar of Hunter's heavy metal.

"Be right here at midnight!" Hunter yelled over the noise. A shrieking bout of laughter erupted from a cluster of girls and somehow pierced the mix of music.

"I'll call you if I find a ride," Daniel yelled back. He gave his brother a thumbs-up, which won a pair of rolled eyes. His bother started pulling away in the Taurus before Daniel had a chance to slam the door. The car's acceleration did it for him.

"Who's that?" someone in the yard yelled at him. "No randos!"

Daniel turned to the house to see silhouettes scattered across the front yard, embers glowing as smokers inhaled. An empty grocery bag buzzed past on a stiff breeze. Daniel looked to the sky behind him and realized it was much darker than it should've been. The feeder bands were already reaching overhead, blotting out the waning rays of the summer's late setting sun. The last Daniel had heard, the storm was moving a bit more north, starting the habitual hysteria in Charleston that had become an annual event ever since Hugo crushed the peninsula two decades ago.

"I think it's that creeper," someone else said, their voice drifting along with the music.

Daniel ignored the smattering of kids in the yard. He weaved his way down a driveway stuffed with cars and headed for the side door. A handful of kids were in one of the cars, bright orange dots flaring out with inhalations, then dying down in a cloud of smoke. Coughing broke out, followed by laughter.

The garage door was open, a crowd spilling out of it. Daniel made his way through. A kid he somewhat recognized from school sat behind a card table, selling red plastic cups for ten bucks. A keg in the corner of the garage couldn't have been getting more attention if it had on a mini skirt. Daniel waved the kid off and squeezed his way inside.

Around the line of girls snaking back from what Daniel assumed was a bathroom, he caught a glimpse of Jeremy Stevens directing traffic. Daniel went the other way, into the dining room where two wannabe DJs had their turntables set up. Wires snaked everywhere; two egg crates full of LPs sat on chairs to either side, and both boys held their headphones to their ears, nodding their heads off beat to what could only be different tunes than the one playing. Speakers stacked in one corner rattled the windows with great puffs of bass. Daniel could feel his shirt flutter against his chest as he walked by. It was too loud to even think in the room. He pushed his way through as quick as he could.

In the next room, Daniel stumbled onto a videogame tournament of some sort. An extra TV had been set up, and eight boys sprawled across sofas and chairs with an equal number of dead-bored girlfriends. Both TVs were broken into four squares, each square with its own gun bobbing in the center, chasing after something to kill. Somebody knocked over a plastic cup full of beer, which led to more screaming and cursing. A girl squealed and clutched her dress.

"Daniel!"

A hand slapped down on his shoulder; Daniel turned to see Roby grinning at him, a plastic red cup in his hand.

"You drinking?"

"Jada's driving," Roby said.

Daniel looked around. "Where is she?"

"Bathroom. Hey, Amanda Hicks is here."

Daniel felt his temperature rise. Amanda Hicks was the first girl he'd ever kissed. Or she, at least, had kissed him. Or something. She was a wolf in sheep's clothing, a vixen who could disappear around school, then leap out while you're waiting on the bus one day and swirl her tongue in your mouth. Daniel was equal parts frightened by and in love with her.

"You want a cup?" Roby waved the yeasty scent of cheap beer in Daniel's face.

"Nah. I told my mom I wouldn't."

"Me too," Roby said, his voice rattling around in his raised cup. He took a long swig, then wiped his mouth with his sleeve. "Hey, maybe the three of us will go swimming later."

Daniel peeked through the living room and out to the partially lit deck. Each time the sliding glass doors opened, they let in the sounds of laughter, of girls squealing, and water splashing.

"I didn't bring my trunks, and besides, we're supposed to get all kinds of rain from that storm."

Roby rolled his eyes. "You're in a pool, asshole. You're already wet. Hey, here's Jada."

Daniel looked over his shoulder to see a girl heading their way, a coy smile on her face. Jada was beautiful. Daniel nearly blurted it out loud, he was so surprised. She wasn't gorgeous, not like a model, she was too short for that. But when he pictured a girl dating his friend Roby, he imagined someone overweight with bad skin and thick glasses. Jada was none of those things.

She stopped in front of Daniel and held out a slender arm, a hand on the end expecting to be clasped. Roby was saying their names to each other. Daniel noted her straight hair, so black and clean it looked purple. She had a normal face, thick lips, a wide smile, and dark eyes that threw out light. Daniel felt her pumping his hand and heard her say something. He was still stunned that his best friend was dating someone not hideous.

"Singing camp, huh?" he asked. He had no idea what he was supposed to be saying.

Jada smiled at Roby. "That's right. Your friend has a powerful voice." She smiled and raised a plastic cup to her lips.

"Aren't you driving?" Daniel asked.

Jada took a gulp and shrugged. Roby slapped Daniel's back and yelled over a sudden bout of excited screaming from the gamers. "She's just gonna have one, and we're not leaving for a while yet!"

Daniel wiped a bead of sweat from his hairline. "I think I'm gonna go outside for a second," he said. The crush of people, the thumping music, the rat-a-tat gunfire from the games—they were stifling the hell out of him.

"We'll meet you out there. I'm gonna go hit the keg again."

Roby and Jada left him there and wove off through the crowd, their hands linked. Daniel felt nauseas. He scanned the throng of laughing, happy, popular people and felt perfectly alone. He really *was* a rando. A creeper. A sketch. He saw himself—for just an instant—how everyone else must see him: cringing from the music, no cup in hand, no girlfriend, no interest in shooting people online. He dug out his crappy cellphone and checked to see if maybe his brother had called. Perhaps their date had been called off for some unknown reason and he needed to pick Daniel up early. But there were no messages. No texts. No funny SMS clips of the latest thing bound to go viral that *he* would be last to discover. All he saw was the time, which let him know he'd only been at Jeremy Stevens's party for fifteen minutes.

Daniel shoved the phone back in his pocket and

moved toward the patio door. He wanted to get outside and let the humid coastal breeze cool his sudden sweat.

The glass doors slid open and burped more laughter, squeals, and wet swimming noises his way. Daniel pushed through the mob choked up by the doors, fought through the cup-holders and dripping bathers, and finally dove between the gaping glass teeth of Jeremy's home, escaping the gullet of his teenage discomfort.

7

A stiff wind chilled the sweat on the back of Daniel's neck, then moved off to rustle in the trees. The concrete patio behind the house was wet from the running, shivering, dripping swimmers. Daniel got out of the way as more people filed through the swish and slam of the glass door. He felt pathetic without anything in his hand and no one to talk to. He shoved his fists into his shorts and tried to look normal. He swore someone in the pool said something about a creeper, and further swore that they were referring to him.

Daniel strolled off to one corner of the patio where there was less light. He then realized that this would do nothing to make him appear more normal.

A girl from his homeroom—Valerie, he thought—ran by in a soaked t-shirt, her lacy red bra visible beneath. The glint of steel from her lip and nose piercings caught Daniel's attention. He had no idea she had them, having never seen her outside of school. As she shuffled around to the pool's steps, he saw that her shirt just came down to her waist, exposing the panties she was wearing for bottoms. A tattoo peeked out between the two at him, like a bashful eye. There was no way she was old enough to get a legal tattoo; he wasn't sure about the piercings, what age you needed to be to get them. Daniel wondered what her parents thought about it all.

As the DJ moved from bass-heavy hip-hop to some rapid trance music, the energy of the crowd intensified. Or maybe it was the wind picking up. Daniel huddled up to the side of the house under a mildewed awning and watched his classmates in their natural environment. He felt like a naturalist on safari.

This is the missing episode of Planet Earth, he realized. They never did a show on the most bizarre life form of them all: *humans.*

A boy one year older than his sister joined Daniel in the darkness, his red Mohawk spiked up tall. He leaned against the wall, slid down to his butt, and started trying to coax a flame out of his lighter, his hands forming a desperate variety of cup and bowl shapes against the wind.

Daniel looked from the triangular spikes pointing up at him, to the kid with the horn-rimmed frames and flat-billed trucker hat, to Valerie's metallic adornments. He looked from the skinny jeans to the baggy pants that were shaped like shorts, but so large and worn so low, they almost went to the kid's ankles. There were girls in glitter, girls with black lips, girls with fake tans, girls powdered to a vampiric pale, kids with spiked collars, with outrageous cowboy beltbuckles, with superhero shirts, with faded logos of products that none of them had been alive for the manufacture of—

And Daniel looked down at himself. He wore a pair of tan shorts that looked like at least a dozen other pair of his tan shorts. He had picked out one of the few t-shirts that was both clean and hadn't been left in a twisted ball to wrinkle. There was nothing hip about his shirt. Nothing vintage. Nothing ironic. It was just plain and dull and normal, like him.

The wind whistled through Jeremy Stevens's back yard, howling through the trees, heard even above the music. Daniel had a sudden realization: he was the only kid he knew who didn't fit in somewhere. And it was because he wasn't even *trying*. He had put no effort into it. A cannonball threw a splash of water his way, and Daniel danced to the side, catching a little on his shin. He laughed and scanned the cliques, wondering which one he could probably belong to. Were there any that didn't require tattoos or needles? Was it too late to try and join a group during his senior year? How would he walk up to the hipsters in a pair of tight pants, the cuffs high above his ankles, a scarf around his neck in August, and explain to them that he was now one of them? Or would he be better off just dressing up and waiting for *them* to come to *him*? That sounded more reasonable. Daniel wondered what Roby would think. Then he wondered what was taking his friend so long to fill his cup and come out and join him. He looked around for the couple and saw, now that he was looking for differences amongst his classmates, what they all had in *common*. One accessory that even the swimmers had, holding them up above the turbulent, rippling water:

Plastic cups.

****

"Ten bucks."

Daniel handed the kid a twenty and took his change. The bill he got back was soaking wet with what Daniel hoped to hell was pool water. He wadded the tenner, shoved it in a pocket, and took his cup.

Someone did a handstand on the keg while Daniel waited in an amorphous blob of a line. Once they were done, several people squeezed through from behind to get topped up, and Daniel realized he'd have to be a little more assertive if he was going to get a drink. He pushed through and held his cup out alongside a cluster of two others—plastic rims crinkling together—while someone showered gold-colored beer in all three and across their knuckles.

Daniel came away shaking foam off his hand. He wiped his palm on his shorts, then realized how that smell was going to linger. He tried to remember if he'd told his mom he wasn't going to drink at all, or if he'd said he was just going to have one. His brother *was* driving, he reminded himself. He took a sip from the cup, foam tickling his nose, and wondered if his brother had also promised not to drink.

"Are you in line?"

Somebody tapped Daniel on the shoulder. He spun around and realized he was standing by the keg, sipping on his beer. A pack of thirsty animals with empty cups were arranged behind him, all of them staring.

"No, go ahead."

Someone mumbled "rando" loud enough to hear, and Daniel wanted to point out that he wasn't random at all. He'd been invited by someone who'd been invited by someone.

"Jeremy Stevens would've taken summer school if it weren't for my best friend," he wanted to shout out.

He shuffled out of the way and back into the house, dodging elbows and potential spills as he went. The number of people in and around the house seemed to have doubled since his first tour through. Daniel rose up on his toes and looked for the distinctive dark curly head of his best friend, wondering where they'd gotten to. He thought of asking people, but could foresee the wrinkled faces and the confused "Who?" he'd likely get from most of them. But hey, at least he had his accessory. His drink. He took another gulp, waved his hand toward the far corner of the kitchen like he saw someone he knew, then squeezed through the crowd in that direction.

Daniel was rounding the center island when someone bumped into him from behind, sending him and a splash of his beer into the girl ahead. Daniel cursed and apologized, but his efforts were drowned out by the girl's startled screams. He reached to brush the foam off her back when she spun around as fast as a tiger—and he smacked Amanda Hicks on the boob, instead.

"What the fuck?" Amanda looked down at her accosted breast, then twisted around like a snake as she tried to reach the back of her shirt. "Was that *beer?*"

"I'm sorry," Daniel said. He pulled his hand back before she could bite it off.

"I'm so fucked," she said. She looked up at Daniel. "You've totally fucked me."

Daniel wanted to point out that the most they'd done was kiss, and just that one time.

Amanda punched his shoulder and stormed off, the crowd parting before her huffed rage like a running of the bulls that had been soberly reconsidered.

"Nuts," Daniel said. He took a swig of his foamy, sorta-cold beer and fought to look inconspicuous. The DJ went back to bass thuds; a plate in the Stevens's kitchen cabinet rattled to the beat.

"Daniel?"

A familiar and piercing voice squealed at him from behind. Daniel turned and saw the last person he ever expected to see at the party. He would've been less surprised to see the girl from the summer before—the second person whose tongue he'd had in his mouth. Instead, he saw his sister, Zola.

"What in the hell are you doing here?" he asked. Both of them looked down at the red cup in her hand, and then at the one in his.

"Don't you tell mom," she said.

Daniel steered her toward the sink where a pocket of reduced jostling beckoned.

"How did you get here?"

Zola peered over her shoulder at her friends, but let Daniel guide her by the elbow away from them. "I was at Susie's and her boyfriend called. We just stopped by so she could see him."

Daniel tried to grab the cup of beer from her, but his sister steered it away from him. She took the opportunity to nod at his cup. "Didn't you tell mom you wouldn't drink tonight?"

"Did I?" Daniel asked. "I thought she said one was okay."

Zola frowned, and Daniel remembered correctly.

"Truce," he said.

Zola nodded. She took a defiant sip of her beer, and Daniel felt some foreign sensation, like seeing a color he couldn't name. He wished he'd hadn't gotten a beer so he could lecture her, or stop her, or feel less like a hypocrite for doing so. He took his own sip instead, feeling suddenly as if he and she were both of an undeterminable age and either a gap had opened between them or had closed. He had no idea which it was, or in what direction.

"Did you get invited to this?" Zola asked, lowering her drink and glancing back at her friends.

Daniel felt a twinge of humiliation. "Roby invited me."

"I *thought* I saw him when I came in," Zola said. "But who invited *him*?" She raised her hand. "Never mind. I don't care." She nodded to one of her friends, who was waving her hand. "I've gotta go. My friends are waiting for me."

"Wait. When did you get here? Have you seen Roby?"

She pointed toward the ceiling. "He was going up the stairs when we came in the front door. I dunno, maybe ten minutes ago?"

Daniel watched as she spun back toward her gaggle of giggling, freshman friends. He peered down at his beer, finished off what was there, realized he was already buzzing and was destined to get grounded for the miserable evening he was having. He went off in search of Roby.

8

Daniel worked his way through the kitchen toward the living room. The stiffening wind outside whistled through the cracked sliding glass door, mixing with the laughter and screams outside. In the living room, the gamers had retired from their eight man tournament and were now watching YouTube videos on the larger of the two TVs. One boy sat on the floor with his laptop, which seemed patched through to the display. Daniel watched a boy on screen jump from a rooftop toward a trampoline, missing violently. The kids on the sofa jumped up and laughed in horror; they clasped their hands over their mouths or pumped their fists.

"You need to get in line," a girl yelled at him, as Daniel started up the steps.

"Excuse me?" He worried he was slurring already.

"The bathroom? This is the line." A girl he thought he knew from one of his classes pointed at the long stream of girls standing on the steps, snaking all the way up.

"I'm looking for someone," Daniel said. But just the mention of the bathroom, and the recently-downed beer, had awakened his bladder.

"I'm watching you," the girl said.

Daniel lowered his brows at her, wondering if she were serious, then began pushing his way up the crowded steps. A couple came half-tumbling down in the other direction, and he had to press into some other kids to let them by. That started a fresh round of complaints and cries of "creeper" and "no breaking."

At the top of the steps, Daniel made his way past the bathroom into all the glorious open space in the hallway beyond. Two kids stumbled into a bedroom and were yelled at by some other kids. They came back out giggling and covering their mouths, hanging onto one another and sloshing beer. Daniel got out of their way as they staggered toward the steps.

"Roby?" Daniel rapped a knuckle on the bedroom door.

"Fuck off!" someone not Roby yelled.

He went to the next room. The door was open a crack. Daniel pushed it open a bit more. "Dude, are you in there? I think I need a ride home."

The bedroom was empty, but a wreck. It looked like Jeremy's room. There were posters on the walls, a jersey tacked amongst them, a shelf lined with trophies. Daniel backed out and looked the other direction down the hallway. The Stevens's house had more bedrooms than his house had *rooms*.

"Hey, you."

Daniel turned to see Amanda Hicks coming down the hall from the direction of the piss line. She waggled her finger at him, and Daniel heard the kids downstairs roar with laughter over one of the YouTube videos.

"Hey, Amanda, look, I'm sorry about the beer—" Daniel waved his empty cup. "Some asshole bumped into me, and then I fell forward—"

"Shutup," Amanda said. She grabbed a handful of Daniel's formerly wrinkle-free shirt in a tight, angry fist and pulled him into Jeremy's room. "Get in here."

Daniel stumbled into the room and the door slammed shut behind Amanda, leaving them in darkness. Daniel could hear the wind outside roaring against the glass and rattling the shutters. He brought his hands up in front of himself to ward off Amanda's attack, but the light beside the bed clicked on instead.

"Are you fucking scared of me or something?" She rested one hand on her hip and smiled at the defensive pose Daniel had adopted.

"No," Daniel lied.

Amanda crawled onto the bed, crossed it on her hands and knees, and turned on the lamp on the other side. She titled the shade to aim more light at him. Daniel could hear the kids downstairs howling with laughter.

"Take off your shirt," Amanda told him.

Daniel looked down to confirm that he was wearing one. His head felt dizzy. He set his cup on the mantle, between a trophy and a teddy bear, and fumbled at the hem of his t-shirt. He wasn't sure why he was obeying, what spell this girl, who had once grabbed him and stuck her tongue in his mouth while waiting on the bus, had on him. He pulled his shirt off and stood there, holding it.

"Drop it," she said. Amanda moved toward the foot of the bed and sat there, on her knees, watching him. Daniel let go of his shirt. The roar of the wind outside and the roars of laughter from downstairs created a dream-like surrealness around him. This wasn't the way he saw the night, or his life, going. But then, he never imagined himself going off to college a virgin, either.

"Now the pants," she said.

Daniel grabbed his belt buckle, as much to defend it as release it. "What about you?" he asked, then realized how unromantic and crude that sounded. It was like he thought their mutual nakedness was something to barter.

Amanda reached for her pants, dug her hand in her pocket, and came out with her cellphone. "I was just gonna watch and take some pics," she said.

Daniel laughed nervously and went to grab the phone from her. Amanda hid it behind her back and threw a hand against his chest.

"I'm just kidding," she said. "I'm turning off the ringer. Just let me text my girlfriend."

Daniel stood there while she jabbed at the thing with her thumbs. He looked back at his shirt, which sat in a crumpled heap below Jeremy's mantle. He wondered what Roby and Jada were doing.

"I meant it about those pants," Amanda said.

He looked back to find her lounging at the head of the bed in a mash of pillows. She smiled at him, looked pointedly in the general direction of his belt, the phone having disappeared from her hands. "Off," she commanded. "Then you get a kiss."

Daniel looked at the lamps on either side of the bed. "Shouldn't it be darker in here?"

"Not if I'm gonna see." She waved her hand at his belt, as if dismissing it from the room.

Daniel went over and locked the door, then came back toward her side of the bed.

"Down there," she said, pointing.

Daniel returned to his spot. He smiled unconvincingly and pulled the tab of his belt through the

buckle, releasing the metal finger from its worn-out
hole in the leather. The belt jangled while he opened the
button on his shorts. Rather than go through the process
a second time, and to avoid Amanda making fun of his
white briefs, he pulled both his underwear and shorts
down to his ankles with one motion and nearly fell over
as his sneakers caught in his underwear. Daniel danced
and yanked one shoe off to free his feet, then regained
his balance. He stood up and threw both arms wide in a
"Ta-Da! Are-you-satisified?" expression.

Amanda smiled, and the unfortunate timing of the
downstairs laugh-track made his testicles seem to shrink
as a living room full of kids laughed loud enough for him
to hear.

"Can you turn around?"

Daniel followed Amanda's eyes and smirk and looked
down at his penis. It was already throbbing just from
the eroticism of being seen naked by a girl. He turned
around, his arms still raised as if airport security had
found a tube of toothpaste in his carry-on. He wondered
if he should be fighting his erection or encouraging it.
More laughter from downstairs helped make up his
penis' mind, if not his.

"That's perfect," Amanda said, as Daniel came
back around to face her. She was smiling at his dick,
which made Daniel wonder what exactly she found to
be perfect. Lord knows, he would love to have some
validation in *that* direction. Like he suspected most
boys his age did, Daniel fretted over the nature of his
penis: the size, shape, curvature, and every little vein
of the thing. As far as he could tell, Chatroullete, a
website that randomly matched web-camera enabled
victims, was designed from the ground-up to facilitate

a large sampling of comparative genitalia for curious male teens. Daniel had spent more than his fair share of time rapidly clicking through the masturbatory feast, wondering if his cock was normal. His conclusion, after hours of impartial research, was that there was *no such thing* as a normal penis.

Daniel and his penis moved toward the bed and Amanda.

"Get the fuck outta here," Amanda said.

Daniel froze. "Do what?"

She leaned forward from the pillows and laughed at him. "I said get the fuck outta here you creep."

"But I thought—?"

Amanda spun from the bed, aimed a middle finger at Jeremy's trophies on the mantle, fumbled for the lock at the door, then stormed outside.

The laughter from downstairs was riotous. Daniel tugged his shorts on and jammed his foot back into his shoe. He snagged his shirt from the floor and shrugged it on. Pulling out his cellphone, he brought up Hunter's number and selected it. He was zipping up his shorts with one hand when his phone beeped with an error.

Daniel looked down at the phone. There was no signal.

"Jesus Christ this sucks," he said to himself. He went out into the hallway and fought his way down the steps, past all the girls with crossed knees. The way his t-shirt rode up on his neck, Daniel knew he'd put it on backwards. The thump of the bass and the clamor of the crowd and the echo of Amanda's laughter made it feel hot as hell inside the house. When he got to the base of the stairs, Daniel heard a round of raucous applause. He looked up from the lack of bars on his cellphone to see everyone in the living room looking back at him, necks craned from the sofa. On the TV, a naked kid stood facing away from a webcam. The boy spun slowly, and a girl who looked very much like Amanda Hicks could be seen on the bed beyond. A boy with a penis very much in the shape of Daniel's rotated past the camera, then kept spinning.

The wind and the laughter roared even louder in Daniel's ears. Somewhere, a teddy bear sat on a mantle, out of place, unblinking, seeing nothing.

9

A billion faces were pointed his way, but Daniel saw his sister's first. The look of raw horror on her face, of absolute disgust, gave Daniel a fever. He wilted. The laughter was background noise to the knowledge that he'd never be able to look at her or ever talk to her for the rest of his life. He wondered how that was going to work out for the next year. He would have to run away from home and skip college. He was now homeless.

Daniel turned and ran toward the front door, his panic pure comedic gold for the others. Cellphones flashed as they captured the moment for all eternity. Daniel fumbled with the door, his mind already racing with how many Facebook status updates he was about to become the featured attraction of. He would never be able to go to school again. He would have to move. Some other family would have to adopt him. His life as he knew it was over.

He finally got the fancy lever on the door figured out, and a gust of air forced it open. The door flew out of Daniel's hands and slammed into the small table in the foyer, seeming as if his rage had done the damage. Daniel pushed out into the wind, leaving the blasted thing open, and looked to his phone again, hoping Hunter would be able to come and get him immediately. His brother was gonna *kill* him for this.

A branch overhead snapped in the breeze. Kids along the driveway were yipping and yelling over the howling wind, clutching their hair and purses. Daniel stood there, waiting for a bar to appear on his cellphone, when a flash of blue lights appeared down the cul-de-sac. A police car rolled up to put an end to the worst party of Daniel's brief life.

Two cops got out, cones of bright white light emanating from their hands. The flashlights spun over the party scene and bobbed their way toward the front door. Daniel froze on the stoop. Inside, he could hear the laughter and fun disintegrate into panicked curses. The stomping of running feet melded with the bass thumps. Faces appeared in parted blinds. Plastic cups rattled on hardwood.

"What's your name, son?"

A searchlight shone in Daniel's eyes.

"Daniel Stillman," he blurted out.

He was naked on Facebook. He was going to jail. His mother would have to get witch doctors to resurrect him, so she could kill him after he had killed himself.

The officer squeezed a device on his shoulder. "We've got the boy," he said, which puzzled the hell out of Daniel.

"Where's your sister?" the cop asked him. The other cop banged on the open door before barging in. Daniel heard him shouting for the music to be turned off, which it quickly was. With the bass gone, the howling wind became clearer and louder. Upstairs, there was the thunder of frightened kids scampering.

"She's inside, I think."

"Stay here," the officer said.

"Is something wrong?" Daniel didn't know why, but he had a sudden pang of fear that something bad had happened to his mom. Why were the officers there for him, specifically?

More blue lights pulled up in the cul-de-sac. Daniel could barely hear the thump of their car doors before more flashlights jounced through the swirling wind and toward the house. He waited on the stoop while cars were cranked, kids piling into vehicles, officers shining lights on faces so that they seemed to hover over the ground, bodiless. A complex weave and shuffle of parked cars began, of kids checked for varying levels of sobriety, of two boys led off to one of the police cars. Someone drunkenly tried to crank their car twice, setting off a buzzing rattle. Jeremy Stevens's party was disintegrating, but with something like a controlled chaos. Like a forced evacuation.

"Daniel!"

He turned to see Roby and Jada sliding out the front door around a cluster of other kids.

"What the hell?" Daniel asked. His mind was still spinning with panic, embarrassment, and confusion.

"They're saying the storm turned, that we need to get home. C'mon, Jada's gonna drop you—"

"I can't." Daniel shook his head. "Zola's here, and the cops are looking for her. They told me to stay."

"The cops are looking for *you*?" Jada asked.

Daniel noticed for the first time that two of her buttons were fastened to the wrong holes, giving her shirt a large, open wrinkle. A wave of jealousy crashed over all the other emotions he was feeling.

"Maybe your parents sent for you," Roby said. He looked out to the end of the cul-de-sac. "They seem more interested in getting us home safely than busting up the party."

Daniel saw that he was right. His mom's car was with Hunter, his stepdad's in the shop, so he had to—

He fumbled in his pocket for his phone. "I've gotta tell Hunter," he said. Daniel vaguely recalled that this was why he'd come outside to begin with. He watched his empty bars, waiting for them to return.

"I've got nothing," Roby said, looking at his own phone.

A branch snapped off up in the trees and crashed into the yard. It sounded even worse and closer for not being able to see it.

"Let's get out of here," Jada said, tugging on Roby's arm.

"You coming?" Roby asked.

Daniel looked back toward the front door. "I can't, man. I've gotta wait for Zola." Daniel looked down at his backwards shirt, the smell of beer ripe from his spill. "I'm so fucked," he said.

"I'll text you as soon as my cell works."

Jada pulled Roby down Jeremy Stevens's front steps.

"You guys be careful!" Daniel hollered after them. He shielded his eyes as a blustery gust churned up the dirt and sandy gravel trapped in the pocket of brick by the front door. More people spilled out and filed past, most of them holding and cursing their cell phones, the fun and excitement drained out of the air, leaving just the howling wind to chase them all home.

10

"I guess my mom called you?"

Daniel sat in the front seat of the squad car. He faced the side window as he spoke to keep his beer breath from puffing over toward the cop. Zola sat in the back, snapping her phone's keyboard open and shut, over and over.

"I'm friends with your dad," the cop said. "We had calls from quite a few concerned parents, actually, so I was heading this way anyhow."

"You know my dad?" Daniel asked. He somehow doubted that, unless fingerprinting had been involved.

"Stepdad. Sorry." The cop glanced over at him. Daniel saw it in the reflection of the window. "Carlton and I went to school together."

"Why won't my phone work?" Zola asked. Daniel turned and saw her leaning forward, her fingers wrapped around the open window of the Plexiglas barrier rising up from behind the seat.

"One of the towers lost power, and there's too much demand—" The officer glanced back at Zola. "There's a ton of people trying to make calls all at once. Don't worry, they're working on it."

"So the storm's heading this way?"

Daniel peered through the windshield at the dimly lit trees bending on the sides of the road. Branches and leaves were already scattered along the shoulder and on the pavement ahead. It looked like any one of the dozen tropical storms and near-misses he'd seen while growing up in Beaufort. The city hadn't had a direct hit since the fifties, hadn't had a major pass since Hugo. This was supposed to be just another windy weekend in an unusually banal hurricane season. Downed trees and lots of rain and excellent surf—

"It looks like it's heading right for us," the officer said. "As soon as I drop you two off, I'm hunkering down with my family. Lots of folk are trying to evacuate, but it's too late to do that safely. The interstate is jammed."

"Evacuate? I thought Anna was heading for Florida."

The officer turned on his blinker and swerved into Daniel's neighborhood. "This morning, it was looking more like Georgia. Then this low pressure north of us pulled it more our way. It's been churning in the Gulf Stream for half a day and picking up steam. They're saying it might be a category three or four when it lands."

Zola stuck her face by the window in the Plexiglas. "I still can't reach anyone," she said.

Daniel spun around in his seat. "Forget about your phone," he said. "Who're you calling after ten anyway?"

"I wanna make sure Monica got home okay."

"We're going to make sure everyone gets home, don't worry." The officer steered into their driveway and hit his siren for half a second, sending out a high-pitched bleep. Lights came on in the foyer, spilled out around the front door, and then their mom was down the stoop, her blazer flapping in the wind.

Daniel popped out the door and walked her way.

Zola cried out at not being able to open the doors. The officer consoled her through the window as he stepped back to let her out.

"Are you okay?" Daniel's mom asked. She grabbed his shoulder and studied his face.

"I'm fine, Mom. It's not like anything's happened yet. It's just a storm."

"Have you been drinking?"

Carlton joined them on the stoop. He hurried down to speak with the officer.

"I had a sip of someone else's," Daniel lied. "Just to taste it."

"Get in the house," his mother said sternly.

"Are either of your phones working?" Zola asked as she stormed up after them.

Their mother shook her head.

"Where's Hunter?" Daniel asked. He filed inside the house as his mom waved them along.

"He's staying at his girlfriend's. I told him I didn't want him driving in this."

"It's just a little wind," Daniel complained. He kicked off his shoes and plopped onto the sofa as Carlton came back inside, shutting the door hard against the wind.

"Is that it?" Zola asked.

Daniel followed her wide eyes and looked toward the TV. It was the weather channel, the word "MUTE" in green letters across the bottom. It showed a satellite image of Anna overlaid with the standard oblong, concentric circles of varying colors. A chart on the side gave wind speed. Daniel ignored all of that. All he saw was the size and shape of the thing. Anna was the size of Georgia and South Carolina put together. As the time lapse went back twelve hours and ticked forward, he watched it grow before his very eyes. It went from a disorganized patch of white with the barest hint of an eye to a killer buzzsaw with a perfect circle in the center.

"Turn it up," he said as Zola grabbed the remote.

The experts at the hurricane center rattled off all the reasons the storm was changing and moving, and some of the excuses for why they hadn't seen it coming. They repeated what the officer had said about the Gulf Stream. They showed similar storms from previous years, even one that crossed Florida twice, stopping in the Gulf and inexplicably reversing directions. "These things happen," they said. "It's an inexact science."

When they went back to satellite shots of Anna, her clouds ticking through the last half day of movement, Daniel could see it deflect northward, riding the warm and upward flow of that giant mid-ocean river off the East coast. A meteorologist drew in the lines of a cold front with a digital marker, showing how it was sucking the storm northward. There was a lot of talk about Charleston and "another Hugo," even though the current track lines had it running right through Beaufort.

"They're worried it's gonna brush Charleston," Zola said.

"But it's gonna slam into *us*," Daniel muttered.

"Zola, help me round up the candles." Their mom hurried off toward the utility room. Zola dropped the remote and went to the mantle to grab the fancy ones.

"What can I do?" Daniel asked, not taking his eyes off the TV.

"I've got the tubs filling with water," Carlton said. How about you filling some containers with some more. Tupperware, buckets, anything you can find."

"For drinking?"

"I'm not drinking out of the bathtub!" Zola yelled

from the dining room. She stuck her head around the corner, a bundle of red candlesticks in her arms.

"Nobody's drinking out of the bathtub," Carlton said. "It's for flushing the toilet and whatever else we might need it for. If we lose power, we won't have the well pump."

Daniel followed Carlton into the kitchen and started rummaging around in the cabinets for pitchers and containers with lids. He noticed a few flashlights and a ton of loose batteries on the island counter.

"So the worst that can happen is that we lose power for a while?" He topped up a pitcher with water and set it on the counter. Carlton fit the lid inside the pitcher and rotated it closed. He slid it to the side and frowned at Daniel as he began filling the largest Tupperware.

"The worst is that we lose the house or someone gets hurt."

Daniel saw that he was serious. "Were you here for Hugo?" he asked. Some things lived in his brain as legend, or historical curiosity. For him, Hugo was nothing more than before and after pictures in Charleston area restaurants. It was commemorated lines on the sides of buildings showing how high the tide got. It was the news clips of boats in trees that they used to scare people into evacuating, convincing families to get on the interstate and sit for twelve hours on what should be a two hour jaunt. In his neck of the woods, Hugo had become the name of the prototypical storm, even though he was sure there'd never be another like it. It was the bogeyman of meteorology. It lived in the weather closet, and parents used it to terrify kids.

"I was in Charlotte for Hugo," Carlton finally said. His eyes seemed to focus far away, his lips pressed together. When he returned his attention to Daniel's face, he must've seen the relief there, for Carlton's guise hardened further.

"It was still an amazing storm, even that far inland. Tornados were spun off every which way. You've never seen so many trees down or houses demolished. Nobody had power for days, most for weeks."

Daniel felt water spill over the lip of the full container. He sloshed a little more out so it could be handled and passed it to Carlton. He grabbed the next one as the window over the sink rattled in the wind, absorbing its fury and shivering with it.

"What do we do next?" Daniel asked. He looked out at the fluttering leaves and the twisting trees in the back yard. He remembered, as a kid once, helping his father put plywood over every door and window when Floyd looked like it might be the next Hugo. It became a category five, the worst sort of storm, but never made landfall. They had done all that work for nothing. And now they had done *nothing* in preparation, and already the wind outside seemed dangerous.

"Now you should go get some sleep. Take a flashlight with you. Your mom and I will wake you up if it gets bad."

Daniel handed him the last container and shut off the water. Carlton squeezed his shoulder. In that instant, and for the first time, Daniel realized Carlton was his own person. It seemed obvious in retrospect, but the thought had never hit him before. This man who had stumbled into their lives, and then their home, had existed *before* he did either of those things. He had lived somewhere else. He had been through other storms. He had been a kid just like Daniel. These were alien thoughts.

"Try and get some sleep," Carlton said.

Daniel patted his stepdad on the arm, even though he felt like doing more. He was just so used to doing *less*. He grabbed a flashlight, clicked it on and off to make sure it had juice, then ran off toward the stairs. He stomped up them, rounded the bannister at the top, and headed for his room. As he passed his sister's room, he saw the door had been propped open with a chair. She was inside, sitting up in her bed, holding her nonworking phone toward the window and grumbling at it.

Daniel laughed at her as he changed into sleep pants and a clean t-shirt. He placed the flashlight on his side table, turned off the light, and rolled over to gaze out the darkened window. Outside, shadows shivered. Trees waved their arms like ghouls, and leaves threw themselves flat against the glass, peeked inside for a moment, then raced off to some hurried elsewhere.

11

Daniel woke to a flashlight shining in his face. At first, he thought it was the cops. He was back at the party. Had he passed out drunk? He was dreaming of being naked at a party with his entire class there, even his parents. Everyone was laughing. Was he being arrested for being naked in public?

"Daniel, I need you to get up."

"Huh?"

He sat up and rubbed his face. He was home. Why was he getting up? Wasn't it a weekend? Was it Monday already?

"Daniel, honey, get some clothes on and come downstairs."

Daniel saw flashlights dance through the hallway outside. He could hear Carlton and Zola conversing. He reached over and twisted the knob on his lamp. It clicked and spun, doing nothing.

"The power's out," his mom said. She pressed a flashlight into his palm before he could begin to think of groping for it. "Put on some pants and some socks and shoes. And bring a pillow."

With that, his silhouette of a mom took her cone of light out of the room. Daniel could hear her rummaging in the upstairs bathroom while he tugged on a pair of jeans. He grabbed socks, slid them on, his head still groggy as he reached for his shoes.

"What time is it?" he asked.

"It's two o'clock."

"Only two?" He'd only been in bed for a couple of hours. He slid a shoe on. Whistling sounds coincided with vibrations throughout the house. He could hear air forcing its way through the tiny gaps around his window. Studs in the walls creaked as the upper floor seemed to move a little. Daniel grabbed his flashlight and raced out of the room, then remembered his pillow. He went back, grabbed it and his comforter, and ran downstairs, trailing the blanket behind.

"Zola?" He waved his light over the living room, but nobody was there. Pillows and a blanket were scrunched up on the sofa, the remote lying on top. It was where his mom and Carlton had played sentry while they slept.

"In the bathroom!"

Daniel walked through to the kitchen and shined his light down the hallway. The bathroom door was open.

"Are you using it?"

"Don't be gross! Carlton's in here."

Daniel went down the hallway, confused. A lambent glow spilled out of the bathroom. He peeked inside and saw candles on the counter. His sister was scrunched up on the tile, between the tub and the wall, a pillow behind her head. She looked upset at having been awakened.

"Are we supposed to all fit in here?" He stepped over Carlton legs and sat down beside his sister. She reached for his comforter and spread it out over her knees.

"This is so stupid," she said.

"It's in the center of the house," Carlton explained. "No windows, and the walls are close together. It's this or sitting in the pantry and hoping the canned goods don't jump off the shelves."

"Why couldn't we just sleep through the whole thing?" Daniel asked. He flicked off his flashlight to save the battery as their mom squeezed into the bathroom. She unloaded an armful of their toiletries by the sink, then sank down with her back to the cabinet door.

"Everyone okay?" she asked.

"Fine," Carlton said. He squeezed her knee. "How're you?"

"I'm not needing this right now," their mother said. She tucked her hair back behind her ear, then pressed both hands against her face. "I'm so behind at work. I did not need this right now."

"So Hunter gets to spend the night at Chen's?"

Carlton threw Daniel a look. "Her parents are there. The officer who brought you two home said it was best not to be on the road if it could be helped."

"How long before they fix the cell phones?" Zola asked.

"Please stop with that," their mom said. Her voice sounded strained.

Daniel frowned at Zola, who pouted and looked near to crying. She flopped over on her side and curled up in a tight ball, knees to her chin, her phone clutched in both hands.

"How long do we need to stay like this?" Daniel asked Carlton.

"Just 'till it blows over," he said. "It could be hours, so if you can sleep, you should."

Daniel leaned back against the side of the tub and hugged his knees. He rested his chin on his kneecap and watched the candles throw shadows everywhere. Upstairs, the house creaked and popped as it moved around on unsteady joints. The wind was whistling louder and higher. Daniel thought about his father, who had built the house many years ago. He wondered if he'd fucked that up like everything else. The thought made him suddenly fearful about the sturdiness of their shelter. Still, Daniel had heard heavy storms assault the house before. It had always survived. As Zola kicked his feet to the side, making more room for herself, he thought about how ridiculous it was for the four of them to be crammed into a single bathroom. He was thinking this as he drifted off to sleep—

****

There was a period before every hurricane where the only things stirring in the air were excitement and anticipation. Daniel had grown up with a series of near misses. He had watched news crews roll through town, had spent entire days in front of the weather channel as track lines were plotted and re-plotted. He had gone to the beach to watch the surfers in their wetsuits paddle out through rushing walls of foam. He remembered standing up on one of the many boardwalks that crossed over the grassy dunes to the hard pack of Beaufort's beaches beyond. The waves were crashing all the way up to the dunes, slicking the sea grasses down like hair on a wet scalp. Daniel had stood at the end of the raised wooden platform and held onto the rail as the angry ocean leapt up, over and over, to crash across his thighs and knees, threatening to sweep him off into the street.

Another time, with the sea not so enraged, he and Roby had tried to swim out through the storm-angry breakers. Even without surfboards in their hands, neither of them had been strong enough to dive down and swim through the powerful currents engendered by the curling waves and walls of foam. There had been a moment during that exhausting swim when the fun and excitement had taken a bad turn. The raw power of the ocean around him, the roar of the foaming and spitting sea, the endless reserves of strength nature seemed to possess as it sent one riled wave after the other, never letting up—Daniel remembered the fun turning to panic.

Swimming out of the ocean, calling for Roby, letting him know that he was giving up, he had felt the largeness of the universe around him. He knew, then, what it was to be a speck floating in the infinite. There was no crying "mercy." It wasn't Hunter, who could be pleaded with. He couldn't change his mind, couldn't beg the ocean to stop, to let up on the roaring foam. As he swam back to where his feet could touch, straining on tiptoes to push toward the beach, the piles of white froth on the surface of the water had gone into his nose and mouth. The ocean was a rabid dog. But as he pressed further, and the walls of crashing wave stopped spilling over his head, then crashing at his back, then pushing against his knees, then lapping his running, high-stepping, shivering ankles, Daniel saw it as something worse than an enraged mutt. It was, instead, a destructive and unfeeling thing. It threatened without *knowing*.

Roby's eyes had been wide and dripping with fear as he joined Daniel high up the dune. They had laughed with nerves and shivered in the strong, chilling wind. The ocean, meanwhile, kept thundering. It was a dozing giant, a disinterested beast that could kill with a sneeze, rattle with its exhalations, strike one down with its barest of shivers. And that, the soulless impersonal giant Daniel saw that day, scared him more than the anthropomorphized monster he used to liken to an angry Earth. He was an ant underfoot. A fly flattened by a mindless windshield. A grain of sand plummeting from a shrugged shoulder and spiraling to its doom—

****

Daniel woke to thunder and the sensation of falling. The house was shaking, his mom crying out in alarm, powder from the ceiling drifting into his eyes as he looked up. He had a sudden image of a wave crashing over their house, of it disappearing in foam, his nightmare images leaking out into the noise and clamor of the *real.*

"What was that?" Zola asked. She sat up and clutched at Daniel. The house was still reverberating from the great crash. The echo of the noise, the sound of it from his dreams—and then Daniel realized the boom that woke them had been much louder than any of the other storm noises. The wind outside was terrifying and loud. It seemed to have grown louder. Daniel could hear the bones and joints of their house cracking and popping, almost as if the nails his father had driven by hand were now coming loose.

Carlton lit a candle. "Sounded like something hitting the house," he said.

There was fear or sleepiness in his voice. Daniel could hear a swishing sound beyond the howl of the wind as sheets of rain pummeled the siding. It sounded like a massive straw broom was being raked violently across the house, over and over.

"Like a boat, or something?" Daniel had images of Hugo in his mind. They were miles from shore and the nearest marina, but he couldn't shake the image of waves crashing over their house, like in his dream.

"Probably a tree."

"Is there anything we should do?" his mother asked. She lit another candle, and Daniel saw for the first time that his all-powerful mom was scared and at a loss. He pried Zola's fingernails out of his arm and patted the backs of her hands.

"Sorry," his sister said.

"Can I take a flashlight and go look?"

His mom and stepdad both frowned at him. "This is the safest place to be until the storm's over," his mom said.

"I've gotta pee," said Zola, bouncing her knees.

"Just a quick look, Mom. Just to see what it was. I won't be long."

Their mother looked back and forth between him and Zola, then turned to Carlton.

"I wouldn't mind seeing what's going on out there," Carlton admitted.

"Alright. We'll move out into the hallway and take turns using the bathroom. Nobody flushes, okay? We'll do that last."

Zola groaned. "Are you serious?"

"And I've got a garbage bag here somewhere for the toilet paper so it doesn't clog up." Their mom dug in the bag of supplies she'd been using as a pillow.

"This sucks," Zola said.

"You're lucky you're going first," Daniel told her. He grabbed one of the flashlights. Carlton flicked one of the others on and back off again. The three of them shuffled into the hallway as Zola lifted the top lid of the toilet, still complaining under her breath.

"Damn, the house is *moving*," Daniel said.

"Watch your language," his mom said.

"We forgot to crack the windows," Carlton hissed. He flicked on his flashlight as Zola pushed the door shut, squeezing off the light from the candles inside.

Daniel turned on his flashlight. "Why would we crack the windows?"

"It's supposed to regulate the pressure inside and out. I don't know if it's an old wives tale or if there's anything to it—"

"My dad used to make us do it as well," his mom said. "They used to say it kept the roof from sucking off."

"Is that what that noise was?"

"Nah, I think that was a tree hitting the house. It probably sounded a lot worse than it actually was."

"We should crack the windows, I think," his mom said, indecision in her voice.

There was a flushing sound in the bathroom.

"I'm sorry!" Zola called out. She cracked the door just as their mom was reaching for the knob. "It was a habit. I couldn't stop myself!"

The toilet gurgled; Zola pouted in the cone of light from Daniel's flashlight. "I'm sorry," she said again.

"It's okay," their mom said. She patted Zola on the arm. "You wanna come out while I go?"

Her eyes darted to the sides as the howling outside intensified during an especially powerful gust. The house swayed. "Can I stay in here *with* you? I won't look."

Their mom laughed. "Okay." She kissed Carlton on the cheek. "I would just crack a few of them several inches or so." She squeezed Daniel's arm. "Be careful and don't be long."

Daniel nodded.

His mom slipped into the bathroom and shut the door. He could hear Zola still apologizing and making excuses inside.

"I'm going to crack the ones in our bedroom first," Carlton said. "I'd like to grab an extra pillow and a blanket and drop them back off here."

"I'll do the living room and then just peek upstairs real quick," Daniel said. "You'll do the kitchen?"

"Okay," Carlton said. He nodded, and Daniel caught the barest of smiles. Carlton tucked the flashlight between his elbow and ribs, clapped his hands once, and said, "Break," like a football quarterback.

Daniel laughed and headed off in the other direction.

As the house rattled in the assault of wind and rain, he stopped laughing and padded along silently, hoping the house wouldn't take his stepfather's suggestion literally.

12

As Daniel crept down the hallway, playing his flashlight across the floor and up the walls, he suddenly felt like he was on patrol. The wild sounds outside made it feel as if he were on a ship being tossed on the seas. He was a lone sailor checking the bilges after crashing onto a reef, seeing how much water the ship was taking on.

It most certainly didn't feel like his house. All the lights were off. As he passed through the kitchen and into the living room, he saw that even the appliances were dead. All the twinkling blips that normally graced their powered-down faces had blinked shut. The place looked abandoned. Condemned.

Daniel stole across the living room carpet toward the windows looking out over the front yard. He set down his flashlight and unlocked the window. Air hissed and whistled through the seams, the wind outside like a passing freight train. With his fingers bent in the jamb, Daniel lifted the window a few inches, and the air burst inside immediately. He had a sudden impulse to slam the window shut as the storm clawed its way inside, but refrained. He figured the whole point of opening the windows was to allow the insides of the house to match the fury outside. He wasn't sure if he was imagining it or not, but he thought his ears had popped like descending in an airplane. He squeezed his nose and blew out, then bent to retrieve his flashlight.

Before he moved to the next one, Daniel pressed the lens of the flashlight up against the window, shining it outside. The pathetic dribble of light did little to wash away the darkness, but he could see several of the trees outside bending in the wind. Unlike before, however, when the small trees had been moving, Daniel could now see the *big* ones swaying. The little ones were snapped in half. He could see flashes of white wood where their raw and exposed interiors caught the light. Brambles of limb littered the yard already, looking like a scattered hedge. Leaves sped by like jet-powered bugs; the wet ones plastered themselves to the house and windows. Rain came in sideways and in blinding sheets, like a powerful sprinkler dousing the house. Daniel felt the water misting him across his thighs as it blew through the screen and the new opening he'd made. It was hard to move away from the window. He was transfixed by the incredible forces powering through their front yard.

Finally, he tore himself away and moved to the next window. He cracked it, then ran to the dining room, bumping into a chair that had been left pulled out from the table. Carlton yelled something from the kitchen, but Daniel couldn't hear over the wind he was inviting into the house. He flashed his light through the windows to look for a tree or anything leaning against the wall. Seeing nothing, he ran back to the living room and up the first few steps toward the second floor, shining his light well ahead of him.

The storm sounded twice as fierce upstairs. It sounded like the roof was off. The howl and whistle were completely unabated, like Daniel would walk up the next few steps and find naked clouds roiling above, leaves blowing through, just a few bits of low wall standing around him.

He took each step cautiously and reminded himself that it would be raining on him and the carpet would be soaked if the roof were actually gone. Once his head was higher than the second floor, he rotated his light around through the pickets of the railing, just to be sure. All the walls were there. Daniel kicked himself for being so stupid and afraid. He ran up the last handful of steps and went straight for his room. Throwing the door open, he first grabbed his book bag, which had his books, schoolwork, and a few comics in it. He slung both straps on and moved to the window.

Daniel peered outside. He could see a second cone of light shining out below where Carlton was scanning the back yard from the kitchen window. If the front yard looked like a war in progress, the back looked like the aftermath. One of the really big trees was down. The sight of such a large cylinder of wood lying flat through the back yard was jarring. Limbs stood up from it like smaller trees sprouting vertically from its bark. These were whipping around like the pom-poms fans shake at the high school football games. As Daniel cracked the window, he saw bits of bark and pine needles, along with the usual leaves, stuck to the outer glass. The air shrieked as he let some in, and the door to his room slammed shut with a loud bang.

Daniel flinched and felt goose bumps run up his arms. He turned around and shoved his bed away from the window to keep it from getting wet. Then he ran around and gathered up the clothes on the floor and threw them on top of the bed. Something scampered across the roof—or a limb tumbled across it—but it sounded like it was right on the other side of the sheetrock above his head.

"This is fucking nuts," Daniel said to himself. He felt a rush of adrenaline from all the pounding and creaking. As the upper story swayed, the image of being on a ship during a storm was complete. He opened his door, feeling the wind yanking against him. He slid his dresser down the wall as he held the door all the way open, pinning its edge behind the furniture. He then ran to Hunter's room and cracked a window there. He wondered what Hunter was going through across town. He always seemed to get out of doing stuff with the rest of the family. Zola's room came last. As Daniel approached her door, he thought he heard squishing from the carpet beneath his feet. He was still processing this when he opened the door and stepped inside—

Something bushed across his face; Daniel screamed and dropped his flashlight. He waved in the air to shoo whatever it was off, and his hands tangled in twigs and leaves. He bent for his flashlight, the spray of rain pelting him. The thunderous roar of the wind was so thick, it drowned out his thoughts. He felt like he'd stepped outside, or through some dimensional rift from his comics and into a hellish, infernal plane of existence.

He shined his light inside as the door banged against his foot. Something ran across the floor and disappeared into the darkness. Splintered two-by-fours hung from the busted-open flesh of cracked and hanging sheetrock. Zola's ceiling fan was on the floor, glass shades and shattered light bulbs glittering—he aimed the flashlight up—there was a tree trunk angled through her dormer, a thick limb splitting her bed in two. Another squirrel ran past, twittering and complaining. Now that he knew what they were, he placed the sound in the attic from earlier. The animals were moving from their downed home and into *his*.

"Holy shit," someone said behind him.

Daniel startled and nearly fainted. He felt Carlton's hand on his shoulder as his stepdad aimed his own light past and added it to Daniel's.

"That's the old oak out front," Carlton said, more awe in his voice than fear. "We need to get downstairs."

Daniel nodded his agreement. The two of them turned and hurried back toward the stairs, the wrath of the storm outside threatening to send another tree their way. The door to Zola's room slammed shut as the wind swept through the house. He and Carlton thundered down the steps, their lights jouncing, their hands sliding along the railing, drowning out the scampering of smaller, no less frightened feet up in the attic.

13

"Dude, your room is toast."

Daniel and Carlton squeezed back into the bathroom, which smelled sulfurous from freshly lit matches. Zola looked to Daniel, her face pinched in confusion.

"It was a pretty good sized tree," Carlton told their mom.

"What do you mean *toast*?" Zola asked.

"You'd be *dead* right now," Daniel said. He didn't say it to torment, more out of shock and awe and from his pounding heart.

"*Dead?*" Zola howled.

"Daniel, don't do that to your sister."

"There're squirrels everywhere."

"Mom!"

"Daniel Stillman!"

"Everyone calm down," Carlton said. He turned off his flashlight and set it on the counter. Daniel's mom was sitting on the edge of the tub; his sister knelt on the floor amid a tangle of pillows and blankets. Her eyes were wide and fixed on Carlton.

"What happened?" she asked.

Carlton lit another candle. "A tree fell into the house,"

he said. He looked to their mother. "It went through the dormer in Zola's room, but it looks like—"

"There're *squirrels* in my room?" Zola howled.

Carlton showed her his palms. "Everything's gonna be okay," he said, but Daniel knew he was just placating her. There was no way to know if everything was going to be okay. How did they know where the storm was exactly? It could still be miles away. The eye wall could be barreling right for them.

"My Zune," he said, shrugging off his backpack and setting it down on the floor.

"Is the house okay?" his mom asked.

"It's holding up the tree, but I'd say the worst of the impact is long over." Carlton paused. "The damage from the rain isn't going to be good."

"The insurance is up to date. I remember writing that check just a few weeks ago. This wouldn't qualify as flood damage would it?"

"I don't think so," Carlton said. "I'm not sure."

Daniel dug in his bag for his Zune. It was yet another humiliation in his life. All his friends had iPods, and every connector to everything in the universe seemed to be designed for Apple's ubiquitous device. His aunt's *car* even had an iPod dock, even though she didn't own one. She had bought him the Zune for Christmas, then asked him to plug it into her car and play some of his favorite music. Daniel had to weasel his way out of telling her she'd bought the wrong thing and had done his best to sound grateful for the gift. He didn't even like pulling it out in public and had bought some white earbuds so it would look like an iPod if he kept it in his pocket.

But it *did* have an FM tuner, something many of the iPods didn't. Daniel had never used it before. He powered it up while Zola begged Carlton for more details about her room. Their mom had to tell her that she was most definitely *not* going up there to see for herself.

"Does anyone know any FM stations?" Daniel asked. He couldn't personally name a single one. The rare times he listened to music in the car, he just tapped the search button from one commercial to the next until he found an actual tune.

"NPR is ninety five point seven," Carlton said. "I think one of the AM stations has a duplicate signal on the FM range somewhere."

Daniel struggled to figure out how to adjust the frequency. *If it was an iPod*, he thought to himself, *it would be intuitive.*

He got the dial moving, the digital numbers ticking down, while he put one earbud in. Carlton patted his shoulder and pointed to the floor. Daniel sat, and Carlton sat down beside him, reaching for the other dangling earbud.

"You mind?" he asked.

Daniel waved his hand.

"That's gross," Zola said, as Carlton leaned close and popped the loose bud into his ear.

Daniel was getting nothing but static. He dialed into the NPR frequency, and there was something there, but it was too faint to make out. He started tapping through the numbers, one decimal at a time, while Zola and his mom dug out bottles of water and passed them around.

"I shoulda charged this thing up," Daniel said, noting the quarter charge on the battery.

"Wait. Go back," Carlton said.

Daniel went up two decimal points. There was a voice behind a curtain of static.

"I think that's a Charleston station," Carlton said, pointing toward Daniel's display.

"Everyone be quiet," Daniel said.

He and Carlton strained to hear.

****

"What did they say?"

Zola dug into a box of cheerios and crammed a few into her mouth. Daniel took a swig of water. Now that he knew the house was open to the elements, the sound of the wind upstairs seemed closer and more potent.

"It's all they're talking about, of course." Daniel looked to Carlton. "Did they say winds up to a hundred forty?"

"That's what it sounded like to me." His stepdad bore a grave expression.

"Where's the storm centered?" his mom asked.

"It was all in relation to Charleston," Daniel said. He wrapped the buds around the Zune and tucked it into his pocket, saving the battery.

"I think it's going to hit just south of us. Maybe right on top of us," Carlton said. "They were saying sixty miles south of Charleston."

"How far away? Is the worst over?"

"It had made landfall," Daniel said, "so it can't be much longer."

"It could get worse before it gets better," Carlton cautioned.

"When can I go see my room?" Zola asked. "Oh my god, my new laptop is up there! We're responsible for those!"

"Nobody's going upstairs," their mom said. "And the school will get you a new laptop if anything happens to that one."

Zola looked nearly in tears. She dropped the fistful of cheerios in her hand back into the box and shoved the box away from herself.

"How long will that radio last?" Daniel's mom asked.

"I dunno. A few hours or so. I've never run it all the way down."

"If there's nothing else we can do, or if you guys don't need to use the bathroom, we should probably get some sleep." Their mom flipped open her cellphone and glanced at the screen. "It's almost four, so the sun won't be up for another two hours. I don't want anyone moving around or exploring before then."

"What will we do if another tree comes through here? Or if the house falls down around us?" Daniel thought about images of demolished homes on the weather channel, the piles of jumbled building material and furniture that nobody could live through. He wondered what it would be like to crawl their way outside in this mess only to search frantically for some place to wait out the storm. Would they have to lie down in a ditch? Or was that for tornados? Would they bang on a neighbor's door like refugees, begging to be let in? What if someone else all of a sudden banged on *their* door and said *their* house had been knocked over and now they had to find room for them and share food and water?

"This is the safest place to be right now," his mom said. She blew out one of the candles Carlton had just lit and rubbed her hand over Daniel's head. "You should try and get some sleep. It'll make it go by faster."

Daniel nodded, but he wasn't sure he'd be able to sleep at all. His heart was pounding from the adventure upstairs. The noise from the wind and rain had him anxious—he felt like a thing constantly under assault and from all directions. But he knew his mom was right. If they were sailors at sea, riding out a terrible storm, they couldn't survive if all of them stayed up for nothing. In shifts and whenever they could, they needed to get some sleep. He moved back by Zola, who had lain down on her side, facing the wall, and had arranged one of the many pillows now piled up on the crowded bathroom floor. Carlton adjusted the extra blanket and pillows he'd grabbed from the bedroom, and their mom blew out the last candle.

Daniel lowered his head. He could feel the cool wetness in his jeans from the water that had spit through his cracked window. He ran a catalog of his stuff through his head—the things in his room that could get ruined if they got wet. For once, he was glad his parents kept the home computer down in the nook attached to the kitchen. All their pictures, documents, emails, home movies, *everything* was on that computer. He had an idea to go out and grab the tower and bring it into the bathroom with them. He was imagining curling up to the unit, keeping it safe, when exhaustion and the late hour won their battle over his racing heart.

14

A great noise had startled Daniel awake the first time—an eerie silence pulled him from his slumber hours later. Daniel sat up and saw that his mom and Carlton were gone, their blankets folded back away from their dented pillows. Zola was making sleep sounds beside him. He rubbed his face to remove the fog from his brain and got up quietly to go search for his parents.

The first thing he noticed was that it was light out, the pale glow of dawn filtering through the windows. Daniel went around the corner and saw that the front door was wide open. He crossed the living room and stepped outside into a different world.

"Holy shit," he whispered, which drew looks from his mom and Carlton. They stood together on the front stoop, her arm around his back, him clutching her shoulders. They had been looking toward the massive tree leaning askance across the front of the house.

Out in the front yard, it was a tangle of limbs. Piles of broken branches formed vast dunes and disjointed heaps of greenery. What was odd was the lack of sound. Not even the birds chirped; there didn't seem to be any fluttering about. Daniel hurried down the steps to look back at the house. The tree that had gone through the roof was one of the biggest in the yard. Three people couldn't have reached around it holding hands.

"Don't go far," his mom said. "In fact, I'd rather you stay in the house."

"Why?" Daniel looked around, his arms raised. "It's over, right? Man, we're gonna be picking up limbs for ages. And how do you get a tree like that off your roof?"

"It's not over," Carlton said. He shielded his eyes and looked up at the brilliant blue patch of sky overhead. Gray clouds stood in the distance. "I'm pretty sure this is the eye. Storms don't end this suddenly. There's just as much wind and rain on the back side of the storm, if not more."

Daniel looked up at the sky. He could see clouds off in one direction, but the house blocked the other. It didn't look like the solid wall of a hurricane's eye like he imagined it should, but then, the woods hid the entire lower half. He was just seeing the dark tops of the storm.

"Are you sure?" he asked.

"Pretty sure," Carlton said.

"The worst part was the last hour," his mom added. "It sounded like the house was gonna blow over. And then it just went dead quiet." She snapped her fingers.

Daniel spun around and took in the utter destruction of their front yard. He heard a cat mew pathetically in the distance. He couldn't see past the tall walls of fallen limbs to see how bad off the rest of the neighborhood was.

"How long do we have?" he asked.

Carlton ran his fingers through his hair. "Depends on how large the eye is and how fast the storm's moving. I hope we don't have long."

"You're ready for it to come *back?*"

Daniel didn't understand.

"I'm ready for it to move *on*. I'd hate for it to stall here."

Daniel nodded.

"Do you think it's safe to run around the house and see how everything else looks?"

His mother shook her head. "There might be power lines down or something else we can't think of. Let's just get back inside."

"I'm going to go upstairs and see how bad the damage is," Carlton said. "And we should try and eat something before the winds pick back up."

Zola appeared behind him, dragging her blanket, which she held wrapped around her shoulders. "Can I go upstairs, too?" she asked. Before anyone could answer, she dropped the blanket and turned and ran toward the stairs. Carlton kissed Daniel's mom and ran after her.

"Sucks about the house," Daniel told his mom. He followed her into the house and watched her close the door and secure the deadbolt.

"It's insured," she said. "I just hate it for Zola. I hope it's not that bad."

"It looked pretty bad."

She waved him toward the kitchen. "I don't want to try the gas just yet, so let's do cereal." She went to the cabinet and drug out a mix of boxes. "We also have these Poptarts if anyone wants to eat them cold."

"How long will we be without power?" Daniel grabbed the milk out of the fridge and shut the door as fast as he could, trapping the cold inside what had become a lifeless cooler.

"It might be a few days, as bad as it looks outside.

And it might look even worse once the other side of the storm gets done with us."

"It doesn't feel like anything's about to happen," Daniel said. Looking out the window, it looked like a normal morning with just some heavy rainclouds on the horizon.

Zola stomped down the stairs with the heft of a mule and burst into the kitchen, crying. She had her sodden bookbag on one shoulder, a stuffed animal in her hand.

"It's ruined!" she cried. She ran into her mother's arms and threw her hands around her back. "Everything's ruined!"

Their mom didn't say anything. Carlton walked in and went immediately for the cereal. Daniel noticed, in the sad and quiet exhaustion on his mother's face, how worn out she was. Her work weeks were invariably draining, but she always had the weekend to recharge herself. A glance out the windows—past the leaves and twigs plastered to the glass and to the debris field beyond—suggested it would be some time before anyone rested.

The light outside dimmed like a curtain drawn over the sky.

"Get some breakfast," their mother said. She let go of Zola and passed her a bowl. Carlton crunched loudly on his cereal and leaned over the sink to gaze up at the sky.

"Make it quick," he mumbled around his food.

An eerie shade fell over the house. A distant howl drew closer. It sounded like wide and fast columns of highway traffic were whizzing nearby. Daniel shook some cereal into a bowl, did the same in the bowl held out by his sister, watched his mom splash some milk on both, then grabbed a spoon from the counter and followed Carlton back down the hall.

"These're the worst winds," Carlton crunched over his shoulder. It sounded more like he was steeling himself for what was to come rather than trying to enlighten Daniel.

The four of them filed back into the bathroom. Daniel and Zola sat in their corner and ate while their mom and Carlton sat on the edge of the tub. An empty bucket floated on the water behind them, and Daniel realized how badly he needed to pee.

There was a crack outside, a sharp report like a canon, and the roar of the wind was right down their necks. It grew even darker in the house, almost as if the sun had changed its mind and slunk back over the horizon, ducking from the storm. The four of them stopped crunching on granola as the pitch and intensity of the wind grew and grew, but still seemed so distant.

And then the wall of hurricane Anna reached their yard. There were more gunshots of snapping trees, audible over the din of the wind. The house shuddered violently as it was hit by the edge of the storm. Daniel felt a surge of nausea clench his stomach. A hollow pit of anxiety and fear of this indomitable thing had returned, much like he'd felt in the surf with Roby those years ago.

The house rattled and creaked. Something snapped somewhere—bits of the roof peeling off, a window shattering, another limb or tree smashing into their home—it was impossible to tell.

The wind groaned through the cracked windows, belching in after them. Daniel could feel the air grow colder, could feel a breeze on his cheeks, could smell the wet rot of disturbed soil and bark. None of them were eating. None were reaching to light a candle. They sat with their spoons in their hands, dripping milk, waiting for the world to end.

"It was like this before, just before the eye came," their mother said. Daniel didn't know if she was trying to reassure them or let them know how lucky they'd been to sleep through it. Daniel thought about how that earlier chaos had just ended suddenly with the eye passing over. This time, it would be another half day of powerful winds clawing at their house, their neighborhood, their entire town. Zooming out, he had a sudden and terrific shift in perspective that made his mind reel. Daniel thought about all the millions of Americans going about their days in other states, glancing perhaps at the weather, asking friends what that storm was named again, marveling at the size and shape of the thing on their functioning and powered TVs . . . and Daniel was in the *middle* of it all. He was terrified for his life in the middle of someone else's idle curiosity. He was one of those numbers people rattled off: so many dead, so many injured, so many without a home, so many displaced, so many orphaned. He was a living statistic.

The house shuddered, and Daniel's brain did the same. He remembered Hurricane Katrina, when he was younger. He had watched the news for two days, marveling at how water could literally burn, at people being airlifted from their homes, and he had been little more than curious and awed.

Closer to home, he thought of the people standing in the storm's eye right then. His neighbors and fellow South Carolinians. What where they going through? What were the winds like in Charleston? Were people in distant Myrtle Beach surfing and laughing? Were people in Florida thrilled and relieved? Were kids watching on their TVs, hoping it would be a bad storm so they could be entertained by the news?

There was a great crash on the other side of the wall near him and Zola, and his sister jumped, spilling some of her cereal. She screamed and moved up against him, groping for his hand with one of hers. Daniel put his bowl down by his feet and wrapped his arms around her. Her spoon and bowl rattled together as she held them with one trembling hand.

"It's okay," Carlton told them. He slid across the edge of the tub. His cereal had been put aside; his hands went to their shoulders. Daniel felt himself and Zola leaning into his strong touch rather than pulling away as they normally might have. Their mother moved to the floor and huddled up close. She rested her hands on their knees, and the ring of touching almost felt like a séance or a blessing before a meal. With all of them quiet, Daniel could hear naked and raw wind and rain in the living room. At least one window had blown out.

The wind continued to rattle the house, but the initial wall of fury gradually dissipated. It slid further inland, tormenting others. What was left was a deafening howl and the hiss of sheets of rain. The goose bumps of fear subsided on Daniel's arms and legs. The four of them unwound from their familial knot of terror. Soggy cereal with warm milk was stirred, but little more was eaten. They took turns in the hallway, watching the trees bend through glimpses out the kitchen windows, while others went to the bathroom one at a time. Daniel saw trees nearly denuded of leaves in the height of summer, their naked limbs whipping, their trunks bent and bobbing. He leaned out to see better and watched as the entire yard swayed in synchronicity, following the furious waves of rain and screeching gusts of wind like seaweed caught in the tide.

Taking his turn in the bathroom was the worst. It was the being alone, the moving shadows cast by the solitary flickering candle, the sound of his family conversing in the hallway out there with the storm. Daniel made the mistake of looking in the toilet as he finished his business.

"Is it okay to flush?" he yelled through the door.

Everyone else had gone. His mom said it was fine. Daniel flushed and was refilling the bowl with a bucket of tub water when his family came back inside.

"I hope Hunter's okay," he said aloud.

"Me too," said Zola.

"The Deng's have a nice brick house. He'll be fine."

Daniel looked to his mom. "You've been to his new girlfriend's house?"

She shook her head. "No, but you can bet I asked about how safe he'd be before I told him he could stay the night."

The rain pelted the living room on the other side of the bathroom wall. More dust fell from the ceiling.

"What if our house goes down around us?" Zola asked. "It isn't brick."

"It won't," Carlton said.

Daniel was pretty sure he couldn't know that. It was just what adults said to assuage children's fears.

"When will I find out if my friends are okay?" she asked.

"Well," Carlton said, "it was about eight hours or so after the heavy winds that the eye got here, so it'll be at least that long again before we're through this."

"And then I'll be able to get online?" she asked.

"Honey, it's gonna take them a while to get power restored—"

THE HURRICANE

"What about my cell phone?"

"Zola—" Daniel started.

"Let's try and get some rest," their mother said. She gathered bowls together and placed them in the bathroom sink. When the house shook, the spoons vibrated against the porcelain. The four of them shifted about like campers in a too-small tent, tugging blankets and pillows out from underneath each other and trying their best to get comfortable.

"There's no way I'm going to be able to sleep through this," Daniel muttered as his mom puffed out the candles.

But as before, he was wrong.

15

He endured the sleep of the sick. It was a sleep punctuated by repetitive awakenings, each more blurry-minded than the last. It was a sleep of sticky sweatiness, of damp pillows, of tossing and turning and being kicked by his neighbors. It was the horrid daytime sleep of headaches and demi-awareness. Dreams started seeming more real—and the dark, stuffy, smelly, noisy room into which he awoke felt less and less true.

At some point in the day, Carlton and his mother moved out into the hallway. They slept with their feet inside the door to keep it propped open. Daniel and Zola stretched out and found new, cool spots on the tile and around the other sides of their pillows. They slept some more to while away the hours as the wind outside became less of a menace and more of a nuisance. The wind was never going to abate. Daniel felt like the noise had moved into their lives, like another stepfather, unwanted and unannounced, and now they would have to get used to it. It felt like a fever that wouldn't go away. And just like when he was sick, Daniel thought about how little he appreciated that time of wellness. He never thought about the lack of deafening wind on a normal day. The absence went unnoticed. When he was sick, he always promised himself he'd never again take for granted being well. But once the fever passed, life continued as usual, and he rarely paused to appreciate his wholeness.

If the wind ever goes away, Daniel thought to himself, *I vow to soak up the silence. The quiet.* He'd let the ringing dissipate from his sore ears, eek from his rattling bones, slide away from the anxious lining of his skin, and appreciate the calm stillness left behind.

He promised.

****

The smell of soup pulled Daniel from the hazy mist of his fretful sleep. He slowly stirred. There was pressure behind his eyes from sleeping at the wrong time of day. He stood and rubbed his face, glanced at himself in the mirror, and realized how dirty and grimy he felt. He could still taste beer on his breath, now stale. He rummaged in the bag of toiletries his mom had stashed below the sink and found his deodorant, his toothbrush, some toothpaste. He slid the former up his shirt and applied some over his sweat. He ran some water over his toothbrush, but the gurgling, hissing drip reminded him of the absence of power—and that he'd just used what was left in the pipes. He brushed as he walked out of the bathroom and turned to survey the damage in the living room.

Carlton looked up from an embrace with his mother. She was facing away from Daniel, but obviously wiping hurriedly at her eyes to keep him from seeing that she'd been crying. Daniel looked away from them and studied the mess in the room. Shattered glass twinkled all across the carpet like spilled jewels. A sheet had been hung from the blinds over the blown-out window, but the wind kept pushing it back, and rain kept filtering down to soak the insides of their home. The entire floor was soaked. Puddles had formed here and there, revealing defects in the otherwise level floor. The TV and stereo cabinet had been rained on for hours and were likely ruined. Daniel looked at his old original Xbox sitting on the floor and wondered if maybe this would be an excuse for him to finally get a newer 360.

He hated himself as soon as he thought it.

"Do I smell soup?" he asked around his toothbrush, trying to change the course of his thoughts.

His mom sniffed and nodded. She hurried past him and into the kitchen, and Daniel followed.

"The gas isn't working," she said. "Carlton pulled the camping gear out of the attic before the storm hit."

Daniel saw that their old Coleman stove had been set up on the island. A worn fuel canister dangled from its curvy pipe. Flames licked and hissed at the bottom of a pot; the clear lid was fogged and bubbling with the steam of warm calories.

Daniel spit toothpaste into the sink. "I could eat that whole thing," he said.

His mom dried the bowls from earlier with a clean towel. Daniel saw a bucket of water sitting by the sink, and realized how primitive their home had become. It was nothing more than a cave, and one that leaked rain.

He tapped his toothbrush on the edge of the sink to clean it and left it to dry. Taking a bowl from his mother, he ladled some soup into it and dug in. Carlton pulled out a loaf of bread and handed him a slice. Daniel didn't even inquire about butter—he took a bite and chewed contentedly.

"Should we wake Zola?" he asked.

"Let her sleep as long as she can," his mom said.

"What time is it?"

"A little after two."

"Man." Daniel shook his head and spooned more soup toward his lips. "When will things get back to normal? Like, when will we be able to get the house fixed? Get power and water back? That sort of thing?"

"It depends," Carlton said, helping himself to soup. He turned down the heat on the Coleman, and the hiss lessened. "It could be that we got the worst of it, that there isn't much damage across Beaufort or any of the surrounding area. If that's the case, they'll be able to concentrate on us and get things back to normal in a few days."

"But that's not what you think," Daniel said between bites.

Carlton frowned. "After we eat, we should try your radio again."

Daniel nodded. He turned as Zola exited from the bathroom, rubbing her eyes and pouting.

"Come get some soup, honey," their mom said.

The four of them ate in the kitchen. Zola sat on one of the stools by the island, but the rest ate standing up. For Daniel, it was from having been prone so long. He suspected it was also out of abject hunger. He was too famished to take the time to get comfortable; and the noise outside made him feel too revved up to rest. There were three empty cans of vegetable soup by the sink, and after second helpings, the pot was scraped clean. Carlton turned the stove off with a click of the knob, and Daniel wondered how many of the canisters they had. His brain was in survival mode.

After the meal, Daniel and Carlton went through the house closing the windows against the rain. The threat of the low pressure sucking off the roof was gone, if indeed there was anything to the myth. Now there was just rain spitting in to soak the carpet and furniture.

Daniel surveyed his room as he fastened the window upstairs. He felt guilty for how untouched it was. The carpet wasn't even all that wet since his room was on the back of the house and out of the direct blow of the wind. Compared to the wreck of Zola's room, it was nothing.

When he and Carlton got back downstairs, his sister and mom were tackling the living room, even as the wind blew a steady thirty or forty miles an hour outside. The glass had been swept up. With a mop and bucket, they worked on getting the puddles up from the fake hardwood floor. They wrung the mops out by hand and chatted quietly while they worked. Carlton mentioned the radio again, and Daniel retrieved his Zune from the book bag in the bathroom.

The same station came in a little better than before. They were still talking about the storm. Daniel and Carlton took an earbud apiece and listened to the numbers. The storm had reached category five status just before landfall, an upgrade after getting some better wind readings. It was still a category three even with the eye sixty miles inland. A clip from the Governor was played; he was already declaring it a national emergency to open up federal funds. There was talk of an evacuation nightmare as last-minute residents from Charleston had clogged 26 and 601, leaving themselves locked in gridlock traffic while the storm dumped rain and hail on top of them. Even though the station was based in Charleston, the name Beaufort came up over and over again. The eye had passed right through the city, nearly at high tide, which had caused massive flooding. Power was out for several counties, wrapping up hundreds of thousands in the same sort of living situation Daniel and his family were experiencing. Hearing about the wide swath of damage, at how many were affected, had Daniel thinking of Hunter and Roby and everyone else he knew. Part of him felt a twinge of excitement that school might be out for part of the next week, plunging them right back into an extended summer vacation. An even bigger part of him, however, was dying to be around his peers to hear their stories. There was some guilt to how giddy he felt; perhaps the sensation was as much from the unusual sleep schedule as from the afterglow of surviving something dangerous. He wrestled with the conflicting emotions as he spent the rest of the day's light working around the house mopping up, collecting shards of glass, and fastening a shower curtain over the blown-out window (which appeared to have been caused by a broken piece of limb, found halfway across the room).

Carlton took Zola up to scavenge more items from her room, which left her in tears once again. There was little to be done to keep the wind and rain out of the room. Carlton grabbed a hammer to beat back some exposed nails where broken bits of roof truss poked down through the shattered sheetrock, just to keep anyone from running into them. Daniel felt like they were all searching desperately for something to do, for some way to burn energy, to beat back the storm, or to save their house and possessions. They had spent nearly a full day cowering and helpless, and now it felt recuperative to do anything at all.

The mood lasted until the sun began to set, which seemed to happen suddenly for summertime; the clouds to the West once again gobbled up the remaining daylight prematurely. The wind continued to blow outside, though abating somewhat each hour. If felt like they'd always lived with it, this new wind. It blew as they ate another meal of soup, the fuel canister on the Coleman sputtering as it emptied. It blew as they congregated back by the hallway to drag blankets and pillows out into more space. The four of them ended up in the master bedroom, which had remained dry. It wasn't so much for safety—the house seemed to have survived and would not get worse—it was more for comfort. It was to be near each other as Daniel and Zola curled up on the floor and their mom and stepdad took to the bed. The wind continued to blow as they fell into another long, dark, and fitful sleep, the house creaking with aftershocks as the family slumbered.

16

Daniel was the first to wake the next morning. His mouth felt full of cotton; his head pounded from getting too much sleep. He extricated himself from the knotted tangle of sheets and covers and padded softly across the carpet, out of his mom's bedroom, and through the house.

The quiet outside was unfamiliar and haunting. Once again, the birdsongs were notably absent. The house had also become lifeless. In the perfect stillness, Daniel realized how much residual buzzing he was used to hearing. The refrigerator normally hummed, but he didn't know that until he heard it *not* humming. The compressor usually clicked now and then, but it hadn't for over a day. There was nobody on the family computer; its whirring fans had fallen silent as well. The living room TV was peculiarly quiet. Normally, at all times of day, someone was vying for control of it.

Daniel padded upstairs and changed into a pair of shorts that were already stained from an art class project. He grabbed fresh socks and changed into a new T-Shirt, then rummaged through his bedside table for his cheapo digital camera. Back downstairs, he grabbed his shoes by the front door and slid them on. He let himself out into the motionless air and heavy calm of Hurricane Anna's wake.

Even though the sun was just coming up, the sky was already bright blue to the east. There wasn't a cloud in the sky, almost as if the storm had swept them all up and dragged them off toward Columbia and North Carolina.

Daniel made his way into the front yard and studied the massive tree propped up against the house. The shingled roof was dented in around the trunk of the tree, the flat plane punctured and demolished. He worked his way through the tangle of branches from another fallen tree to admire the peeled-up root ball of the old giant oak. A wall of soil stood up from the yard, held together by the tree's tangle of roots. Where they had been pried up from the earth, a deep depression lay full of several inches of Anna's rain. The void of the missing roots formed a massive bowl, like a giant spoon had descended from the heavens and taken a bite out of their front yard. Daniel fished his inexpensive digital camera out of his pocket and took a picture of the mud-caked wall of roots, marveling at the way the ends had been torn from the violent ripping of the tree's demise. He took a picture of the tree resting against the house, the missing dormer making it appear as if the façade were winking at him. As he panned the camera to take one of the littered yard, he noticed movement in the house. His mom opened the front door and looked out at him, shielding her eyes with a crisp salute.

"I'm gonna look around the neighborhood," Daniel said, his voice sounding much too loud in the post-storm calm.

"Don't go too far," his mother said. "And be back before lunch."

Daniel waved his consent and turned the camera off to conserve the battery. It was already low, and he realized how poorly he'd planned for the storm. His cell phone, his Zune, his camera, and who knew what else was inadequately charged. As much as Daniel mocked others for being reliant on their gizmos and for having far too many of them, he felt his own connection to that digital pipeline now that it had been ruptured.

The driveway was almost completely free of downed trees, but was lined on either side with crashed and crushed limbs. The long arms of the oaks sagged broken on the ground. The magnolia leaves, waxy and bright green, were tangled everywhere. Daniel strolled past them to the middle of the cul-de-sac and turned to marvel at the destruction. The white and yellowing flash of tree-wound was everywhere visible through the mangled canopy of woods. Each spot of raw and splintered yellow highlighted another limb broken, another trunk snapped in two, another tree destroyed or crippled. And the undergrowth was now a tall field of oddly green branches and bushy leaves. It looked like a blind barber had descended on the neighborhood with a gigantic set of clippers, buzzing the trees at random, making a mess of everything.

Through the tangles, Daniel could see more rootballs standing up on end like walls of caked mud. Each one had a large tree attached, the trunk resting along the ground and terminating on a jumbled cauliflower of leaves. Somehow, the trees were larger at rest than they had seemed pointing up at the wide sky. Daniel took a picture of one downed tree that had clipped a neighboring tree, slicing it pretty much in half. He saw lots of smaller trees that had fallen, only to be caught in the crook of another tree's arms. These angled trunks stood out everywhere once he looked for them. He powered his camera off and heard a screen door slap shut somewhere. Through the new jungle, he could see the neighbors from across the cul-de-sac walking across their front yard to survey the damage to their own house. Daniel waved when they spotted him. He didn't recognize either one of them and didn't know their names.

He turned away from the heavily wooded cul-de-sac and wandered up the street, fighting the urge to take pictures of everything. Two houses down, the lone tree in an otherwise cleared yard had fallen against a neighbor's house. The thick trunk hadn't made a direct hit, but the massive kraken of limbs had ensnared the house. The gutters hung like a twisted, glittering tassel from the edge of the roof. The front door was completely hemmed in from the crash. Daniel hoped the back door was obstruction free, or the occupants were going to be climbing out windows.

Several of the houses he passed stirred with the same sort of early-morning activity: People standing outside in pajamas, some of them clutching steaming mugs, all sporting bewildered eyes. They waved at Daniel and each other, and he marveled at how few of his neighbors he recognized. Somewhere in the distance he heard a chainsaw buzz to life, the throttle worked over and over as it revved up and down with the cough of a machine long asleep. Daniel welcomed this intrusion into the quiet. It was the sound of a thing *working* and of progress being made. Somewhere, a piece of the littered ground was being cleared. When he looked out at all the incredible damage, he wondered if it would be months or even years before they had a handle on it all.

"Hey you."

Daniel whirled around and looked for the person calling out.

"Over here."

Someone by the bushes of the next house was waving at him. Daniel turned and walked toward the house. He noticed a huge swath of shingles had been ripped from the roof, leaving the black tar paper underneath torn, a layer of raw plywood exposed beneath that. The person by the bushes waved him over hurriedly. Daniel broke into a jog, wondering if someone was hurt. When he got closer, he saw the person was kneeling down by a solar panel, an open toolbox by her feet. It was difficult to peg the girl's age. She had her hair tied back and covered with a red bandana; her face was plain and young-looking with no makeup.

"Can you hold something for me?"

Daniel shrugged. "Sure. I guess."

He bent down and studied what she was doing. She immediately went back to work, not bothering to introduce herself. Daniel found the behavior odd and somehow intriguing.

"There's not enough wire to twist together, so I need you to hold it while I solder them." She pointed to the two pieces of wire, one of them sticking out of the base of the solar panel, the other coming from a stripped wire that led to a small black box.

"Okay," Daniel said. "I'm Daniel, by the way."

"That's awesome," she said. "Just hold that one right there so it overlaps with the bit of wire coming out of the red part."

"What're you fixing?" Daniel grabbed the one wire and held it close to the small piece of wire coming out of the solar panel. Tracing the severed cord leading away from the panel, he saw that it headed out toward a row of landscaping lights scattered among the bushes and aimed back at the house. He wondered why it would be urgent to get the mood lighting going in the middle of the morning, right after a major storm.

"I'm not fixing anything," the girl said. "I'm *making* something." She held up a small wand-like device that had a butane cartridge shoved in one end. The thing hissed, and smoke curled from the tip. With her other hand, she held a coil of silver wire, one end of it straightened and sticking out like an index finger from a fist. She dabbed the smoking tip of the wand against the coil of wire and some of it melted and coated the end of the device. She then bent close to the solar panel and touched the wand and the wire to the connection Daniel was making. With a few deft touches—her hands were much more still and confident than Daniel's—the joint was made solid, a bright touch of solder reflecting the morning light before it cooled and lost its sheen.

"See if that's gonna hold."

Daniel tugged the wires, and they held fast.

"One more," she said, pointing to another pair that had been stripped back. Daniel was sad there was only one more to do.

"What exactly are you making?" he asked.

"A very weak power station. I think." She smiled up at him before leaning close and coating the wires with another neat connection. Daniel waited for the solder to dull as before, then tested it.

"You're good with that."

"My dad's into radios," she said, as if that explained how she had become proficient as well. She twisted a knob on the soldering iron and set it on a stand propped up in the grass. She pulled out a roll of black electrical tape and began covering the new connections with tight coils. "My name's Anna, by the way." She smirked up at him. "I'm thinking of changing it."

Daniel laughed. "Yeah, that's not gonna be the most popular of names for a while." He rested back on his heels and watched her work. "What's your middle name?"

"Florence."

She laughed, and Daniel joined in.

"That's no good either," he said.

"I know, right? That's a name I'm keeping in the wings until I'm seventy or something."

"Definitely a name to grow into."

She put the tape away and moved to the small black box. After adjusting a knob on it, she flicked a switch and a dim red light glowed. She pulled a multimeter from the toolbox and unwrapped the pair of red and black wires from around it.

"What's this gonna do?" Daniel asked. He couldn't see the solar panel running anything huge, like a fridge or a coffee maker.

"The panel puts out twelve volts for the lights," the girl said. "There's a voltage regulator and a battery in that box mounted below—the one with the wires." She pointed with one of the leads from the multimeter to the new connections they'd made. "This is an inverter my dad uses in his car. It plugs into a cigarette adapter and puts out one hundred twenty volts like a normal outlet, just not as much juice." She bent over one of the small outlets in the black box and inserted the two long, needle-like leads from the multimeter, each one into either of the two slots. "This thing is used to getting nine volts, and now it's getting twelve. Now I need to see exactly how much we're getting out of it in AC."

Daniel smiled. He looked across the street as a couple started dragging limbs from one unnatural pile and placed them in one they had decided made more sense.

"One hundred twelve," Anna said. She sniffed. "That's plenty." She turned a knob on the multimeter with several loud clicks. "Now to see how many amps." She frowned at the LCD readout as it flicked with numbers. "Not bad," she said. "Enough to charge a cellphone or a laptop."

Daniel beamed. "That's brilliant," he said. "What're you hoping to charge with it?"

Anna looked up at him, a lopsided frown of confusion on her face. "Whatever needs charging," she said.

"I know, but what did you have in mind to wanna get up and do this first thing in the morning? A radio?"

She laughed. "No. Actually, we have one of those hand-cranked kinds. No, I didn't make this for anything I've got. They're saying we could be at least a week, maybe more, without power. This'll be for whoever needs it." She pointed toward the end of the driveway. "I'll put up a sign in a little bit to let people know it's ready."

"How much?" Daniel asked.

She tucked a loose wisp of hair, so fine Daniel couldn't tell what color it was, behind her ear. "What do you mean? You mean *money*?" She frowned. "I can't charge for this."

Daniel felt like an ass. He rubbed his hand over his camera, which was low on juice. He'd been asking in order to offer something in exchange for the charge. It had come out like he was accusing, or even encouraging her for gouging people in a time of need, rather than offering them a service.

"I didn't mean it like that," he said feebly.

"Yeah," she said, sounding unconvinced. "Anyway, thanks for your help. Hope I didn't use up *too* much of your time." She rubbed her hands on the seat of her pants. "In exchange for your services, I can let you use this anytime you like." She smirked at him.

"Thanks," Daniel said. He looked up as a man exited the front door with a folded blue tarp in his hands. "I guess I'll go."

"Anna?" The man peered down the driveway.

"Over here, Dad." She waved at him, but looked over her shoulder to smile at Daniel.

"There you are. Whatcha working on?"

Daniel walked down the driveway as she repeated her explanation of the gizmo. Somehow, the fact that she'd done the project without telling her father added to the allure. As Daniel walked slowly toward the next house, he glanced continuously over his shoulder at the two of them, bent down over the solar panel sticking out from the bushes. Instead of continuing his planned walk to the end of the neighborhood and out to the main road, he circled around Anna's house, noting the damage to the shingles, the fruit tree toppled in the back yard, the tall radio tower tangled with limbs. As he wandered back toward his own house, walking slowly by hers, he saw a ladder up against the gutters, Anna and her father scrambling up the roof on a different ladder hooked over the peak, a blue tarp unfolding between them.

Who in the world was this Anna girl that lived four houses down from him?

17

Daniel returned home to find the cleanup around his house already underway. His mom and Carlton were dragging a massive limb down the driveway as he rounded the mailbox. There was already a small pile along their edge of the cul-de-sac.

"There's some oatmeal left," his mom said. "Probably still warm."

Daniel nodded. "I'll be right out to help."

He waved to his sister, who waved back, a too-large leather glove flopping on her hand. She bit her lip and went back to wrestling a small limb, trying to extricate it from a labyrinthine tangle of a dozen mangled trees.

"I'll be right back," he called to her. As he considered the amount of work ahead of him, he couldn't help but feel a tinge of anger toward Hunter. His older brother always seemed to weasel out of laborious tasks. Daniel imagined him sleeping late with his girlfriend, her parents actually out of town, their power miraculously working, a hot tub bubbling under its insulated cover as it waited patiently for long days of lounging, soaking, and doing nothing.

Daniel glanced up at the enormous tree that had stove in the roof. As he bounded up the front steps, he marveled at how normal and everyday that tree and its destruction were becoming. He pictured them getting completely used to it, leaving it where it was, his sister's bedroom becoming a modified treehouse that she shared with the squirrels. He laughed to himself as he raced up the stairs and to his bedroom.

When he opened the door, he found piles of his sister's stuff arranged along one wall in his bedroom. Daniel groaned. He went to his closet and dug around in a drawer of electronics and miscellaneous wires until he found his camera charger. He pocketed that, went to his bedside table, and unplugged his cell phone and Zune chargers from the wall outlet behind it.

Daniel wrapped the thin cords around each of the chargers and hurried downstairs. He retrieved his book bag from his mom's room and stuffed the chargers inside, along with his camera and his Zune. The cell phone he kept in his pocket. Satisfied, he went to the kitchen, hung his backpack from the back of a stool, and helped himself to cold and congealed oatmeal. He gave the microwave wistful glances as he ate for pure sustenance.

Back outside—his stomach growling from the tease of a minimal breakfast—he joined the others in doing what little they could to undo the damage from the storm. Carlton had found some tools in the shed that might help: limb clippers, a wood saw, a hacksaw. Daniel looked at the larger trees lying like a lost game of Jenga all across the yard and realized how arbitrary and useless their efforts were going to be. Chainsaws buzzed in the distance like insects. Daniel knew they'd have to lure one or two of them over to get anything done on their yard.

"How's the rest of the neighborhood?" Carlton asked as the two of them worked to pull a limb from the tangle.

"Lots of trees down," he said. "One against the house next door, but not as bad as ours. Shingles off everywhere." He started to say something about the girl and the charger, but refrained for some reason. He didn't want to mention her even though he couldn't stop thinking about her.

"Did you see any cars moving about? Any work trucks or utility trucks?"

"No. There were people out surveying the damage, though. And I did see one of the power lines down. A tree came down right across it."

"When's Hunter coming home?" Zola asked, voicing what Daniel had been thinking.

"I'm sure he'll get here as soon as he can. They're probably working to clear the roads as we speak." Carlton glanced over at their mom, who had turned away and removed her gloves to get something out of her eye. "We might want to prepare ourselves that it'll be tomorrow before he gets home."

"Maybe Zola can stay in his room until he does?"

Carlton frowned and gave Daniel a look. Daniel bit his lip and dropped the discussion.

They worked and chatted until noon, the late summer sun creeping overhead and drawing the sweat out of them. They drank nothing but water, leaving their supply of canned sodas and cartons of juices for later. The Tupperware containers and pitchers Daniel had helped fill were emptied first, poured into glasses with the last bit of ice from the freezer. They enjoyed the clinking luxury and refreshing coldness before the lack of power melted such things away.

Midway through the afternoon, as the pile of debris along the cul-de-sac grew wider and taller, Daniel started thinking about all the things he took for granted and would have to go without, possibly for days. The internet and cell phones were the most obvious. He was dying to get in touch with Roby, to call or e-mail him about the girl with the soldering iron and unfortunate name. As used as he was to not hearing from his friend over the summers, being suddenly cut off from him right as school resumed felt unnatural. It was also crazy that they couldn't get in touch with Hunter. The entire concept was bizarre. His brother was probably no more than fifteen or twenty miles away, but it might as well have been thousands. Daniel knew, in the back of his mind where logic slumbered, that twenty miles wasn't too far to walk and that some people even chose to run or bike such distances for pleasure, but it felt like an endless, impossible trek to him. He would drive around a parking lot looking for the closest spot, investing more time in the irrational pursuit than the time it would take to cover the extra distance by foot. He never pointed out this inherent silliness when his family left one shop in a strip mall, got in the car, then drove through the parking lot to visit a store just seven or eight doors down. All that seemed normal and natural. Walking fifteen or twenty miles as a means of locomotion seemed absurd. The prior hundred million years of four-legged scampering and eventual bipedalism couldn't compete with the last hundred of flexing an ankle and steering. Not yet, anyway.

"That was the corner with the DirecTV dish on it."

Daniel snapped out of his ponderings and looked to Carlton. He was peering up at the tree resting snugly against the house. "I think it got crushed," he said. He wiped his brow and went back to work sawing a too-big branch in half with a handsaw.

"How are we gonna take showers tonight?" Daniel asked.

Carlton stopped sawing. "Hadn't thought about that." He pinched the hem of his shirt and used it to wipe the sweat dripping from his chin. "I reckon we'll be sponging off from buckets out here."

"*Outside*?" Zola asked, listening in to their conversation.

"The upstairs tub is empty," Daniel offered. "We could take buckets up there and rinse off."

"We'll have to conserve the water," their mother said. "We need to assume it'll be a week without power. It could be even longer."

"There'll be places we can go if it gets to be that long," Carlton said. "After Hugo, they had generators running at the YMCA and we stood in lines for hot showers. But still, we'll have to be careful with how much we use of everything."

Daniel absorbed those words and thought about how surreal their lives had become, and in an instant. He could actually picture what the end of the world might be like. He felt he was getting a hazy glimpse of Armageddon.

"It'll get better once we get a car back," their mother said. "Once Hunter shows up, we'll go try and find some supplies, see if we can borrow a chainsaw, find someone who can get that tree off and patch the roof, even if temporarily."

"Can we get your car out of the shop?" Daniel asked Carlton.

He shrugged. "We'll have to run by there and see."

"There is *so* much I need to be getting done at work," their mom said out of nowhere. She tugged off her gloves and rested her hands on her knees. "This couldn't have happened on a worse week."

Carlton rested his saw on the tree in front of him and went to her side. "There wouldn't have been a good week for this," he said. "When are you not busy at work?" He put an arm across her shoulders, and Daniel and Zola looked to each other in the uncomfortable silence. Chainsaws buzzed in the distance, but it was getting so Daniel hardly noticed them. They were the new sounds to replace the chirping birds, who still had not returned from wherever they had gone. Daniel was waiting for them and Hunter to return. He was waiting for some reason or excuse to visit Anna down the street, even though the idea of just walking to her house filled him with nervous jitters. He was waiting on these things— but it was a surprise visitor who came to him first. The visitor arrived that afternoon as the sun was beginning to set and dinner was being scraped off dishes and into the yard.

It was then that Daniel's father came home.

18

The unexpected arrival of their dad brought the same bittersweet sting and salve that his departure had wrought. The excitement came from the sight of a power company truck, one of the bucket machines with large tires and metal tool cabinets everywhere. Its brakes squealed to a stop in the cul-de-sac; Zola turned to the window, saw it first, and let out a squeal of excitement.

"We're gonna get power back!" she said.

She left the dishes to dry on a towel spread across the dining room table and ran toward the front door. A chair squeaked on the wood floor as Carlton got up to follow her out. Daniel hurried after them, hoping to hear some news from the outside world besides the Charlestonian static from his Zune.

Zola was halfway down the driveway when she stopped cold. The passenger door had opened, disgorging a man familiar at any distance. She stood there, frozen in place, as he shrugged a green duffle up on his shoulder and walked toward them, smiling.

"Frank," Carlton said, more out of stunned recognition than by way of greeting.

Their father nodded. "Carlton."

"What are you doing here?" their mom asked. She moved briskly down the driveway, past Daniel who had taken a spot by his sister, his arm moving around Zola's back. The driver got out of the truck and slammed the door, then rummaged in one of the tool boxes.

"I had no place else to go," their father said, lifting his hands. The smile on his lips dimmed, then faded altogether. "I lost the boat," he said quietly.

Their mom raised a hand to cut him off. She walked past him, toward the man from the power company, who rounded the truck with a chainsaw in his hand. Everyone else stood on the driveway, casting uncomfortable glances.

"How long before the power's back?" Daniel heard his mom ask.

The man shook his head and rubbed the back of his neck. "Can't say," he said. "We're just doing a survey right now." He walked up the driveway and set the chainsaw down by their father's feet. "I told Frank I'd drop him off since I was heading near here anyway." He jerked a thumb over his shoulder. "We came in on our service road by the lines. I think you guys are cut off, but somebody will probably be by in a day or two to let you know more."

"In a *day* or two?" Carlton asked. "How bad is it out there?"

The man frowned. "Governor's calling it a national disaster. They've got trucks and men heading this way from as far away as Florida, but coordinating it all is gonna be a nightmare. Columbia got hammered. Storm went right up twenty six. The entire interstate is closed down while they get it cleared of trees. Hell, it took us all day to work our way over here."

"Is anyone going to bring food or water around? Are the stores open?"

The power man looked to their mother. "Most people who'd be working are too busy tending to their own mess." He glanced toward their house and the massive tree resting across it. "Believe it or not, you guys are lucky. I wish I had better news, but I don't want you guys to plan for the best and be disappointed." He patted their father on the shoulder, nodded to the rest of them, then took a step away. "Somebody will be around in the next day or two," he said again.

Daniel watched his mom run after the power man. "If you and Frank are friends, take him home with you."

The man shook his head. Daniel heard him say something about inlaws, a full house, as much of a favor as he could repay, and then a door squealed on twisted hinges and slammed shut on the rest. The power truck roared to life and did a tight turn in the cul-de-sac. A guilty hand waved from the open driver-side window.

"I'm sorry to do this to you," their father said as their mother stormed up the driveway. Daniel and Zola hadn't moved. It was all playing out like a scene from a daytime drama.

"You're in the toolshed," their mother said. Daniel could tell at once that she actually meant it. She stopped by him, bent and retrieved the chainsaw, then stood back up. "The chainsaw can stay in the house."

With that, she marched back toward the front door, past a frozen Carlton, the silence blooming as the distant buzz of chainsaws fell still and the Beaufort sun set over the first day of Hurricane Anna's aftermath.

****

Daniel slept fitfully that night. He thought of his father out in the toolshed, curled up in a sleeping bag, and his guts twisted with a mix of worry and anger. When he wasn't dwelling on that, his thoughts turned to the girl down the street. Anna, who had smiled up at him as they'd partnered to build—to him at least—a near magical device for sipping juice out of sunshine. The back and forth—feeling infatuation one minute and rage the next—had him spinning in his bed, searching for comfort. Daniel was dying to run to either of them, to wake his dad or Anna up and have some sort of conversation— but to say what? A storm had blown through his life and somehow had left these two people behind like fallen oaks. Both had appeared out of nowhere, even though one seemed to have lived a few houses down for quite some time, and the other was probably just a short drive away for who knows how long.

Twice in the night, Daniel went to his window and looked out over the moonlit back yard—still jumbled with downed trees—and out toward the toolshed in the back. It was one of those prebuilt units, made to resemble a small house with two little windows in the front, a covered porch, and brightly colored trim. Daniel had helped clear a spot for his father inside, twitching his nose at the heavy smell of gasoline, checking the plywood floor for any sign of rat droppings, feeling sorry for him and hating him at the same time. He stood by the window both times that night and looked out at the barely discernible toolshed, then went back to his jumbled sheets and tried to find some solace in them.

In the morning, he woke to the sound of a chainsaw, buzzing like an alarm, but much closer than the others had been the day before. Daniel crawled out of bed and tugged on some bluejeans, despite the sticky heat in the powerless house. His legs had been scratched to hell by the yard work the day before, and it wasn't like he could sweat any more than he already would. The jeans, at least, would offer some protection.

He pulled on a fresh T-shirt and padded downstairs. The front and back doors were propped open, along with all the windows, allowing a slight breeze to plow through the heat and humidity. The roar of a chainsaw chewing through wood rattled through the house. Daniel hurried out to the front stoop, expecting to find his father manning the machine over a thick log, buried up to his knees in sawdust. As he scurried down the steps, Carlton looked up from the limb he was cutting, his safety goggles fogged with an early sweat. He powered the chainsaw down, the chain clacking in complaint, and smiled up at Daniel.

"You want a turn?" Carlton lifted the chainsaw and held it out toward Daniel.

"I'm actually scared of those things," Daniel said. He looked across the yard for any sign of Zola or his mom, but it looked like Carlton was the first one out to work on the storm debris.

"They're completely safe if you use the right precautions." He jerked his chin. "Come here and I'll show you."

Daniel patted his stomach. "Lemme get some breakfast first." He looked back toward the house. "Where is—? Is my dad up?"

Carlton lifted his goggles and placed them on his forehead. "Haven't seen him," he said.

Daniel nodded. "I'll be back in a little bit."

He turned and went back up the steps and into the house. As he crossed into the kitchen, the chainsaw roared back to life and began chewing through more wood. Daniel grabbed two cups from the drying rack by the sink, filled them with room-temperature water from a pitcher, shook a shiny pair of Pop-Tarts packs from an open box, and stuffed them in his pockets. He cradled the cups of water and headed toward the back door. Before he made it out, his sister appeared at the bottom of the steps, her eyes thick with sleep. Zola took one look at Daniel as he prepared to back through the screen door with the cups of water, and knew where he was heading. She gave him a disapproving frown.

Daniel wanted to say something, but didn't. He pushed the screen door open with his heel and backed onto the patio, allowing the springs to clap the door shut. He turned and weaved through the labyrinth of downed trees toward the toolshed. A path through the limbs and brambles had been made by someone else, probably Carlton rummaging for tools the day before. Several other chainsaws could be heard throughout the neighborhood. Daniel's mind drifted toward the girl a few houses down as he stepped up to the toolshed's porch.

He knocked twice and opened the door.

Light spilled through the two small windows. A puff of gasoline-laden air hit Daniel and tickled his nose. His father looked up from where he was crouching on the floor, forcing a sleeping bag into a tight roll.

"Daniel!" His father beamed. The smile on his face was not that of a man who hadn't seen his son in over a year.

"I brought you something to eat," Daniel said dryly. He set down one of the cups by his father's bedroll and fished in his pocket for a pack of Pop-Tarts. "Here." He held them out.

"I've actually been awake for a while," his dad said, almost defensively. He accepted the food and sat back on a pillow Daniel recognized as belonging to the living room sofa. "I didn't want to wake you guys and couldn't really get started with the saw 'cause it was inside."

"Carlton's using it," Daniel said, jabbing a thumb toward the door.

"I heard." His dad looked away. "So, things are going well? How's school?"

The questions made Daniel want to scream, to yell at his father, to beat his fists on something, to run to a girl down the block that he barely knew and press his face into her shirt and cry like a fool—

"Fine," he said instead. "We'd only been back a few days before the storm hit. So I guess I'm acing all my classes so far."

His father laughed. More than the joke warranted. He tore open his Pop-Tarts and patted the bedroll at his feet. "Sit," he said.

Daniel remained standing. He took a sip from his own cup of water, his eyes not leaving his father. He drank a deep gulp, and then lowered the cup.

"I take it you were in the area when the storm hit?"

His dad looked away, as if the truth had scurried into one of the toolshed's dark corners. "I've been living on the houseboat down in the City Marina," he said.

"You've *been* living there?" The water sloshed out of Daniel's cup as his hand shook. "How long? How long have you been here?"

"June?" His dad said it like it was a question, like he wondered how much Daniel's hatred of him would grow if he tossed that out there.

"Were you gonna call? Were you—what was your plan, exactly?"

His dad took a bite of the cold Pop-Tart, crumbs sprinkling down on a nice shirt that hadn't been worn to do nice things in quite some time. "I've been working through things," he said. "I got to where I needed to be close to home to get any better. I just wasn't there yet."

"You needed to be *close*." Daniel tasted the words and wished he had something stronger than water to wash them down.

"I've stopped drinking," his dad said, almost as if he could read Daniel's mind.

"Lemme guess—ever since the storm closed the liquor store down?"

His dad looked down at his tired boots. "It's been since June," he said.

Daniel stepped back toward the door. He turned a bucket over and sat on it, then dug in his pocket for the other pack of Pop-Tarts. He chewed on one dry corner and on his dad's words.

"I really was working up the courage to see you guys. I promise." He looked past Daniel and toward the house. "Is Hunter—?"

"At his girlfriend's since the night of the storm."

"Girlfriend?"

Daniel shrugged. He wasn't about to tell his dad about his brother's relationships.

"Zola looks good."

They chewed their Pop-Tarts.

"Why did you come here?" Daniel asked. "I'm sure you have other places you coulda gone."

His dad took a sip of water. "I guess I couldn't handle not knowing if you guys were okay. If the house was okay. Before, I mean I used to cradle the phone for hours, you know? I'd dial the number and just rub the send button and think of how easy it'd be to press it and hear your voices, even if you were just yelling at me. You were always that close—hell, I was always that close to doing it, but then the storm hit. My boat—" The old man looked away, the morning sun glistening in his eye. "When the marina went, I thought I was a gonner. All of 'B' dock tore loose and surged into town. It was a mess. There were only a few of us dumb enough to be there, and we were lucky no one died. The boats, though—"

Daniel's father fell silent. The chainsaw out front bit into something thick and struggled.

"I'm glad you didn't die," Daniel said. It was as much as he could be thankful for. "I'm gonna go help Carlton. You can—" Daniel wasn't sure what his dad could do.

"I might work back here, just clean some stuff up around the yard. If your mom will let me, I'd like to look at the roof."

Daniel peered at the rest of his Pop-Tart, no longer hungry. For some reason, he wanted to tell his dad about the girl down the street. He didn't know why. He waved goodbye rather than say anything and turned out of the toolshed, breathing in the fresh and gasoline-free air outside. As he walked toward the house, he saw Zola's face pull away from the kitchen window. The chainsaw in the front yard whined as it finished its work, buzzing through open air, the throttle taking it to dangerous places before it was released and wound itself down.

19

Daniel walked around the house, through the destruction and quiet desolation left in the hurricane's wake, and realized how quickly he was getting used to this new environment. The limbs of old oaks, the bramble of foliage, the scattered shingles and wet clods of insulation sucked from broken homes. It was a new normal. The world had been roughed over and changed by the storm.

Rounding the garage, he found Carlton and his mom struggling with heavy logs chopped free from the torso of a fallen giant. Daniel headed for the front stoop, where a pile of work gloves lay beside two plastic cups of water, neither cup sweating with the promise of a cool, refreshing drink within.

He tugged a pair of worn leather gloves on and went to help haul more of the seemingly endless supply of firewood to the swelling debris pile that now meandered partway around the cul-de-sac.

"You okay?" his mom asked, obviously aware of where Daniel had chosen to eat breakfast.

"I'm fine," he said. "Where's Zola?"

"Bathroom," his mom said. She looked over his

shoulder and lifted her chin toward the door. Daniel turned and saw his sister coming out on the stoop. She padded down the brick steps and knelt to sort through all the too-large gloves. Daniel looked back to his mom.

"Is there something we should be doing to get in touch with Hunter?" he asked.

She smiled grimly, her eyes twinkling. "Like send up smoke signals?" Her voice was full of sad impotence, not humor. She wiped her brow with the back of her arm, both of which were peppered with bits of bark and fine sawdust. "All we can do is trust that he's okay," she said. They'll have power or cell phones or something up before long."

"Maybe the landlines still work," Daniel said. He had been against them getting rid of the old house phone the year before, but since it no longer rang, and everyone in the family carried a phone in their pockets anyway, his mom had decided that the cost of the bill no longer made sense.

Carlton returned from another Sisyphean trip to the debris pile. "The landlines weren't working as of this morning." He nodded toward the house across the street, the one with the morning coffee drinkers that Daniel had waved to the day before. "The Morrison's have been trying theirs hourly."

"When did you meet them?" Daniel's mom asked.

"They were out this morning. I checked to make sure the chainsaw wouldn't disturb them. They understood wanting to get an early start, what with the heat and all." Carlton picked up the saw and flicked a lever on its side. He reached into the breast pocket of his short sleeve button-up and extracted his plastic safety goggles. "They seem like good people," Carlton added, and Daniel felt less alone and silly for not knowing anything about them. He thought about another person he'd met in the neighborhood that he'd like to get to know better. The day before, working in the yard, he'd wracked his brain wondering how to get out of debris duty and what he'd say if he went over. By the time he'd worked up the courage and memorized a few excuses, he was too hot and sweaty to want to be seen. As he carried another cut log to the growing row Carlton had started between two trees, he realized he should go over there early and get it over with. Just to keep from perseverating about it all day long or waiting until he got nasty with sweat.

He turned back to his mom as the chainsaw sputtered then roared to life once again.

"I need to run down the street," he yelled. His mother turned from watching Carlton wield the saw, her face scrunched with worry.

"What for?" she yelled back.

A fountain of fine dust sprayed out of the growing gash in the tree; it filled the air with a dry and pulpy mist.

"I need to charge my Zune so we can hear the news," he said, stepping away and squinting his eyes at the fog of powdered tree.

"Charge it how?"

The saw made it through the bottom, and the tree leapt up as another heavy log fell from its end. Carlton looked poised to lop off another, but powered the tool down when he saw they were trying to have a conversation.

"There's this gir—" Daniel realized he was yelling over the residual din of the now-quiet saw. He lowered his voice. "Someone down the street has a solar panel rigged up that can charge small devices. I was gonna go plug in my Zune and let it charge while we work." He looked to Carlton for support.

"Can it do cell phones?" his stepdad asked.

Daniel shrugged.

Carlton dug into his pocket and held out his iPhone. "The charger's on the table by my side of the bed," he said.

"Can you do my Blackberry?" his mom asked. There was a sense of desperation there that Daniel wasn't used to seeing from his in-control workaholic mom.

"I guess," he said, wishing he hadn't said anything. He should've told them he was going to go smoke cigarettes, or something.

"You know where my charger is," she said simply.

Daniel accepted the phone. He was surprised both of them were carrying their phones around, even though there'd been no signal since the storm.

"Check with Zola," his mom said.

"Mine's fine," his sister said. She tugged on a branch. "I put my other battery in."

"Why do you have two batteries?" their mother asked.

Zola shrugged.

"I was already hesitant to ask about charging up my Zune," Daniel complained. Which was the truth, but not for the reason he was insinuating.

"See if they need to borrow the saw in return," Carlton said. He used the hem of his shirt to wipe sawdust off his glasses, which he then pinched with his gloves and inspected.

"Or if they need water. Or anything," his mom said.

Daniel nodded, suddenly thrilled. The idea of making a *transaction*—from one family to another—released the knot of nerves in his stomach. He ran inside for his backpack with a surge of confidence. He was now going on a *mission*, not a tryst. This was about *survival*, not puppy love. He was a sanctioned ambassador with messages and offerings from a not-too-distant familial municipality. There was no pressure to fall in love, or force someone else to reciprocate. All he needed to do was establish a trade route. More formal treaties and arranged marriages could wait.

Daniel gathered his family's dead gizmos and the various species of chargers with their fat heads and wispy tails. He ran back outside, balancing haste with the fear of stirring an unseemly sweat, and made his way through his new and wondrous wilderness neighborhood to that distant and promising kingdom a few houses down.

****

The neighborhood streets were everywhere hedged with brush piles. They were like slumbering and camouflaged beasts, lying supine along the pavement's shoulder. They crowded the black tar, which was still littered with leaves and the smallest limbs, and were deathly quiet and devoid of traffic. While Carlton's chainsaw dimmed behind him, several others became audible elsewhere. The smell of tree sap and tar and sawdust filled the air. As far as Daniel could tell, *this* was the new way of things; the world had reverted to some primitive state, and that's where he'd live forever. Juxtaposing this idea with the fact that people in Atlanta and Chicago were getting up, checking their email, going to work or school, waiting at red lights, hunting for WiFi—Daniel imagined what a Bahamian, Haitian, Mexican or Cuban might feel about such distant and magical realms as the United States. As he rounded the small tangle of limbs in front of Anna's house, he considered the ridiculous idea that he could just walk from this primitive new island of his to that faraway land of promise. A few days of hiking, of sleeping under the stars, and he'd arrive somewhere to find streetlights and air-conditioned houses. There'd be music and roving vehicles. There'd be *signals*: cell phone and wireless, radio and satellite. He could *call* people . . . just not anyone back here.

Daniel wandered up the white concrete driveway feeling conspicuous and uninvited, but also primal and in some survival mode that ignored taboo and embarrassment. He was on a mission from his family, he reminded himself, and nothing more.

As he turned down the walk curling from the driveway, he passed a curious addition to the house that had been erected between two large bushes: a small shed. It had a metal roof bent out of a single corrugated sheet with the solar panels mounted on top. The sides consisted of scrap vinyl siding, and it had double doors on massive hinges that stood open. There was a sign above the doors that read, in a neat print: "Community charging station. Help yourself."

Help yourself, Daniel thought. Did that mean he didn't have to ask? But now he *wanted* to ask.

He peered inside the structure to see the black inverter he'd helped solder mounted to one wall, out of any threat of rain. The other side was lined with shelves that each had their own outlets, which were wired up and covered with electrical tape. A scattering of wall warts were plugged in here and there. Two of them had devices attached, little green lights glowing happily.

For Daniel, it was like seeing a neon sign go up on his little island. He was a caveman peering into a fire.

He saw at once that the same ingenuity and restlessness that had drug his species out of their caves and down from their trees to the twenty-first century couldn't be excised by a storm and a loss of power. Besides, it was his people who had *created* that power in the first place. And now he was seeing a small piece of evidence that it would all come back. Eventually.

Movement inside the house startled him out of his optimistic revelry. Daniel straightened and turned toward the door. Despite the welcoming hand-lettered sign, he wanted to make sure it was okay, especially since he had so many items begging to be recharged.

Lumbering up the stairs, he found the front door propped open, a screen door shut against the bugs. Daniel knocked on the wooden frame of the door.

"Coming!" he heard someone say. Daniel heard feet stomping through the house. He remained on the stoop and adjusted his backpack.

A tall man with a smiling beard arrived at the door; Daniel recognized him as Anna's father, or at least the man who had interrupted their soldering and had been working with her on the roof.

"Is that Daniel?" the man said. He pushed the screen door open and Daniel stepped back and out of the way.

"Yessir," Daniel said, stunned that her father knew his name. *But that meant she's been talking about me*, Daniel realized. His heart leapt with the idea that this lovely sprite with magical powers of soldering had uttered his name—

"Ah, yes," her father said. "I asked Anna who her little helper was, but all she had was a name. Come inside. I'm Anna's father, Edward."

Daniel digested all that information, feeling himself sink and deflate as he did so. The conversation between father and daughter took a more realistic aspect: *Who was that?* A shrug. *Some creeper named Daniel.*

He suddenly felt like bolting through the screen door and sprinting down the street.

There was thunder on the stairs, followed by the squeak of bare feet on clean floors. Anna ran around the corner, her longish brown hair twirling behind her in fine wisps. "Cool," she said, beaming at Daniel. "You brought your stuff?"

Daniel hooked a thumb in his backpack's shoulder strap. The fear and hesitation he'd felt from the risky visit melted. It was as if Anna had been expecting him, or at least anticipating his return.

"Just a few things," he squeaked.

"Bring 'em outside," she said, hurrying past him and throwing open the screen door. "I'll get back to my studies in a little while," she called to her father.

Daniel smiled meekly at Edward, lifted his palms in a shrug, then turned and pushed open the door that had just cracked back on its springs against the jamb.

"Let's see what you got," Anna said. She crouched by the open doors of the little shed and waved her hand impatiently. Daniel hurried over and set his backpack on the walk. He rummaged for each device and paired them with their chargers.

"A Zune, eh?" Anna picked up his music player and squinted at it, then looked up and squinted even harder at Daniel, like she was looking past some glaring flaw to see if she still approved of him.

"I woulda pegged you as an iPod kinda guy."

The way she said it made it sound as if she might've disapproved even *further* of that.

"What do *you* use?" Daniel asked.

"I don't really do music," she said. She tucked a loose strand of hair behind her ear and stared at Daniel. He saw for the first time that her eyes were green. He memorized that in case there was ever a quiz between them, some marital dispute about how little he truly knew her.

She turned away and reached inside the small house. "Looks like you two are done." She unplugged the two devices on the shelves and moved them to a separate waiting area.

"Are those yours?" he asked.

She shook her head. Her hair was so fine, it laid so silky flat on her head, that Daniel could see the shape of her skull beneath. He admired the way the back of her head curved out like a bowl and swept back to her neck, which was half exposed by the parting curtain of brown locks. Her skull seemed loaded with brilliant nerve endings, like Daniel could just cup it in his hand and feel the electrical shocks zap his palm.

"They belong to the Michelsons across the street," she said, turning to face him. "My dad has a cell phone, but he hasn't even tried to turn it on." She held out a palm and curled her fingers. "Lemme see your chargers."

Daniel handed them over one at a time. Anna took the time to check the back of each, reading out the wattage and nodding.

"What were you saying about studies?" Daniel asked. "Is your dad making you do schoolwork?"

"Yeah." She nodded. "School might be closed for you, but mine's still standing." She glanced up at the brick face of her house.

"You're *homeschooled*?" Daniel asked.

Anna frowned. "You say that like I belong to some kind of satanic cult."

Daniel laughed. "I'm sorry. It's not that, it's just that I was wondering why I've never seen you around school."

"Oh." She studied the last power brick. "Four point two watts," she said, "so you have a total of just under seventeen."

"Is that bad?" He couldn't believe he was crouched down so close to her, that they were just *talking*, like they'd always known each other.

"It's fine. I think the panel and inverter can handle around twenty." She looked up at the sky, which was scattered with only the barest of gossamer-thin cirrus clouds. "I'd say these'll be done by lunchtime or a little later." Daniel handed her the cellphones and Zune one at a time, and Anna inserted the plugs that fit each one.

"So I should come back around then?" Daniel pictured coming over and grabbing the devices without her help. The thought depressed him. He looked across the street at another house full of people he didn't know. He thought it was likely that a good-looking boy lived there who was also homeschooled and was Anna's boyfriend. He felt the dangerous urge to ask her if she was seeing anyone—

"Come back at noon," she said. She stood up and rested her hands on her hips. Daniel fumbled with the zippers on his backpack, then slung the now-light sack over his shoulder. "If you want, you can eat lunch with us," she said. "It's nothing special. We're just having some salad to use up the tomatoes and cukes that survived the storm." She frowned. "Of course, you don't have to, you can always just pick up your things whenever—"

"Of course," Daniel said. "I'd love to." He nodded. "Noon." He couldn't remember the last time he'd had a salad, much less as an entire meal, but it sounded like the most appetizing thing in the world right then.

Anna smiled. She held out her hand. Daniel grabbed it and felt her pump his arm up and down. "See you then," she said.

20

Daniel practically skipped home, his hand and cheeks burning. The sweat from the humid Beaufort air stuck his shirt to his chest and back, but hardly bothered him. The awkward goodbye, the way Anna's perfect eyes had darted about while waiting for him to accept her invitation, the handshake: Daniel was thrilled with the stiffness of it all. It was like every stuttering encounter he'd ever had with the opposite sex, but this time it had been mutual! She was almost as awkward as he was.

He ran past one of the brush piles and breathed in the air of injured timber and tree sap. He was pretty sure he was in love. His legs felt at once light and powerful with it, as if he could run a marathon. His brain tingled with the newness, the feeling of being let in to some august and exclusive club. He suddenly knew what so many others must've known for much longer. He could feel his hatred and envy of Roby dissipate. Even as he no longer cared about the storm's aftermath or the loss of power, he desperately wished for some temporary line of communication, some way to tell his best friend that he was no longer a loser for not having a girlfriend and that Roby was lucky to have someone as well.

"Oh my god," Daniel said to himself, slowing to a walk. "I'm losing my fucking mind."

Some girl had invited him to share some salad for lunch, and now he was wondering if it would be better, for their future family, to have a boy first or a girl first. There were good arguments for both ways. An older brother could look after his sister, or he could torment her. Daniel was moving right past losing his virginity to wondering what kind of parent he'd be.

"I'm a fucking idiot," he said to himself.

The deflated sensation intensified as he entered his cul-de-sac and saw his father hoisting a massive limb before letting it flop down on top of the growing debris pile. Daniel used the bottom of his shirt to wipe the sweat from his forehead. As he started up the driveway, he scanned the yard for his sister, but didn't see her anywhere. His mom was also absent. Carlton had moved off to another tree with the chainsaw; the last tree had become nothing more than a dashed outline of its former self, a line of sawdust marching down the row of jumbled logs. Daniel waved at Carlton as he peered up at him through his safety goggles. His stepdad pointed in a tall arch as if over the house, signifying perhaps that the rest of his family was in the back yard.

Daniel dropped his book bag by the garage and hurried around to the back of the house. Yet another pile of twisted limbs lay jumbled at the end of the drive. His mother and sister were just beyond it, talking to one another, their gloves off.

"Am I interrupting?"

Daniel walked slowly in their direction. Zola turned her back. His mom wiped at her eyes and shook her head.

"You guys need any help back here?"

"We're fine," his mom said, which was the opposite of how they looked.

"How long is he gonna stay?" Daniel asked, taking a guess at what was upsetting them.

"He says he has a friend in Charleston he can stay with," Daniel's mom said. "So just until the phones work or he can get a ride some other way."

"And we're gonna make him sleep in the toolshed until then?"

"He's *not* staying in the house," Zola said, her voice as broken up as the tree out front. She kept her back turned; her hands went to her face. Their mom stepped closer and put an arm around her shoulders. She looked back toward Daniel.

"I think there's more for you to do in the front yard."

Daniel let out a sigh. He hated being excluded, but he thought he understood their wanting to be alone. "He says he's quit drinking," Daniel told them. It felt like a feeble attempt. His mom glowered at him over her shoulder, her brow wrinkled and lips drawn tight. Daniel turned and headed back around the house, his elation from a few minutes prior completely and utterly smashed.

For the next several hours, he barely saw his mom or sister. It was only when he was dragging something down the driveway, walking backwards, that he might catch a glimpse of them working slowly and methodically on their brush piles in the back yard. He and Carlton and his father worked with few words. They alternated between disentangling limbs and hauling them to the street, and stacking the green firewood Carlton chopped up between a rare pair of still-standing trees.

When the chainsaw ran out of gas, Daniel's father offered to get more out of the toolshed, but Carlton waved him off and insisted on going himself. That left the two of them, father and son, piling logs, the yard silent of the tree-chewing machine, the distant buzz of a few other saws and the chirping of some returning birds to keep them company.

"I'll be moving on just as soon as I can," Daniel's father finally said. "I hate that I've brought so much tension here." He threw a log on the pile. It landed with a solid and ringing clunk.

"So the boat's gone?" Daniel asked quietly. He remembered days anchored out on the river with the old houseboat. His dad would grill out on the roof while he, Hunter, and Zola trailed behind on the swift current, clinging to fenders and life rings strung out on chewed lines and suspect knots.

"Yup," his father said, then cleared his throat. He turned and wrestled with one of the biggest logs, almost as if to punish himself.

Daniel remembered helping him toss the lines on the boat that last time. When his father had puttered down the intercostal waterway over a year ago, Daniel had watched from the dock and had suspected they were both gone forever, boat and father. Now one of them was back in his life. The other sounded as if it had been demolished in the storm.

"I hope Hunter gets back before you go," Daniel said. He wasn't sure why he wished that, but he did.

"You picked out a college? Or are you gonna go to the community center with Hunter next year?"

"Probably go with Hunter, unless I get some kind of scholarship. My grades are good enough, but they want you to have all these other things. Club memberships, community events, summer camps, volunteering and whatnot." Daniel shrugged. "I'm taking my SATs again next month before I send some more applications out. I'm hoping I can get some money from Wofford if USC and the College of Charleston turn me down."

His father nodded and threw another log on the ever-higher wall of circular bricks. "You dating anyone?" he asked.

Daniel laughed. He felt close to telling him about the girl down the street, but already his delusions of their status felt ridiculous. He didn't even want to explain why he wouldn't be around when the rest of them were eating canned ravioli for lunch.

"Not really," he said.

"Probably best to wait until you see where you're living next year," his father said, almost as if consoling him.

Daniel felt like arguing, like saying a year was too long to be alone—he felt with a burning rage that he needed to *not* be alone. Then he thought of what his father must've been doing the last year, how hard the last few months of sobriety—if he'd really been able to manage it—must've been like. He felt like yelling at his dad for being down at the docks all summer and never calling him. An entire summer of being alone and scrounging for things to do. All those days they could've taken the boat out on the river, the wasted days when he hadn't known some gorgeous girl lived just a few houses down, an entire summer wasted doing nothing when so much had been so close by.

"Whatcha thinking?" his father asked. He looked Daniel in the eye. "Or do I not want to know?"

Daniel shrugged. He looked at the tall pile of logs shouldered between the two trees, dappled light filtering through the gaps. "We should start a second pile," he said. He thought about how rarely they used their fireplace in the winter—mostly just for ambiance around the holidays. Normally, they picked up a bundle of split wedges at the grocery store, a cloth handle stapled to one of the logs, and paid who knows how much for one fire's worth. What they had stacked, once it was split and dried, would last them for decades. It would be sold with the house, he suspected. More than once, probably.

"How about over there?" His dad pointed to two other lucky trees, which would soon hold the remains of their fallen kin.

"Looks good," Daniel said.

He picked up one of the larger logs before his dad could. Carlton came around the corner with a red canister in his hand, a dark mass of fuel and oil sloshing around in the lower half of it. The three of them fell back into their silent routine, working against the backdrop of the roaring and chewing chainsaw. Now and then, they would take breaks and drink warm water from the cups on the stoop. When Daniel did so, he marveled at the idea of the three of them doing yard work together. There was no force in the universe, he would've thought a week ago, that could have coerced him to do half as much with either man, much less willingly.

21

Daniel's mom took the news of his lunch plans in stride, her face showing more shock and bemusement than any pain of abandonment. Daniel used the excuse that he had to go back for their phones and his Zune, anyway. After stripping off his sweat-soaked clothes and sponging off with some soap in the upstairs tub—a bucket of downstairs tub water at his feet—he toweled off, pulled on a fresh pair of shorts and a new shirt, grabbed his backpack, and sped out the front door. The smells of heating tomato sauce faded behind. Outside, as he strolled through his neighborhood, a different smell greeted him: it was the smell of campfires, of burning wood. More than one rising column of gray smoke beyond the trees of his neighborhood signified the beginning of the great fires it would take to remove the debris. It was funny. Daniel had imagined someone would be coming along to scoop up the limbs and leaves. He never considered they might be having bonfires up and down his neighborhood, sending the ash up to chase away the clouds that had felled them.

He turned down the now familiar driveway. The address on the mailbox was 2238. Daniel memorized this, filing it away with brown hair and green eyes. All he needed was Anna's last name and date of birth, and he could practically picture her driver's license. He wondered if she were the sort of person to donate her organs once she was through with them. Seeing a neighbor at the charging station, retrieving a freshly charged device, made him think she probably was.

Daniel waved to the gentleman standing by the solar panel, his phone powering on and giving him reason to frown. He started holding it up to the sky, searching for a signal, while Daniel bounded up the front steps.

He knocked on the screen door, and a man inside yelled, "Come in."

Daniel pulled the screen door open and slipped inside. He wiped his feet, made sure the door didn't slam on the jamb, then followed the sound of cabinets opening and closing toward the kitchen. Anna stuck her head around the corner and smiled at him, then disappeared again. Daniel walked back to the kitchen to find the two of them chopping vegetables on either side of a sink, the open windows letting in what little breeze stirred outside.

"Smells good in here," he said, meaning it.

"We picked a lot of stuff out of the garden before the storm hit," Edward said. "Good thing, too, because the garden flooded."

"You want to snap peas?" Anna asked.

"Sure," Daniel said. He went to the sink to wash his hands, then realized the habitual gesture was futile.

"The tap's right there," Anna said. She pointed to a garden hose snaking through the window and tied down to aim at the sink. Daniel put one hand under the nozzle and squeezed the large, plastic trigger. A thick stream of warm water gurgled out. He rubbed some soap on his hands then rinsed them one at a time.

"How much water do you have?" he asked. He leaned close to the window and tried to trace the hose as it disappeared up and out of sight.

"Oh, we've got tons," Anna said. "I'll show you later. You'll love it."

Daniel smiled at her and thought about how shallow the word "love" was when used in such a way. To suggest that he loved ice-cream was now tantamount to heresy. It was a word reserved for a specific function, and none else.

I'm being an idiot, he thought, in a sudden bout of rationality.

"How bad was the storm for you guys?" Daniel asked. He started snapping the tips off the peas and placing the unused bits in a large bowl of vegetable scraps.

"The house held up okay," Edward said. "We lost some shingles, and our fruit trees out back aren't gonna make it, but I'd say we were very lucky. Especially since no one got hurt." He finished slicing a tomato and held out a piece to Daniel.

"Thanks." Daniel popped the thick, meaty hunk of dripping redness in his mouth and nearly fainted. "Damn, that's good," he said. "Pardon my language," he added, and the other two laughed at him.

"There's nothing like a fresh tomato," Anna said. She nodded out the window toward the large garden with its vine-covered trellises and tomatoes growing up large wire cones. Daniel saw peas on webs made of string and what looked to be corn stalks bent over from the wind. Some of them had been propped back up. "Unfortunately, we lost a lot of good stuff that we didn't pick 'cause they weren't quite ripe."

"Didn't think the storm would be *that* bad," Edward said. He swung the knife in Daniel's direction and bounced it once or twice. "I saw the tree that caught your house. Nasty wound, that."

Daniel popped peas two at a time and set them in a pile with the rest. "Yeah," he said. "There's no telling when we'll get that thing off or get the roof fixed. It went right through my sister's bed. Felt like an earthquake."

"How old's your sister?" Anna asked.

"Fourteen. She's a freshman. My brother Hunter is two years older." He watched as Anna sliced small mushrooms into perfect cross-sectional bits with a tiny razor-sharp knife. "What about you? Just the two of you live here?"

Anna tucked some hair behind her ear, a tic Daniel was madly fond of. She nodded. "I have a younger brother, but he lives with my mom in Pennsylvania." She finished the last mushroom and scraped the slices into a massive bowl already full of lettuce, some other greens Daniel didn't recognize, green peppers, onion, and other buried layers of goodness.

"Is that where you guys are from? How long have you lived here?" He added the peas to the mix. The tomatoes were kept separate. Anna's father grabbed two large spoons and began tossing the salad while Daniel followed Anna's lead in setting the table.

"We're all from Atlanta, actually," she said. She looked to her father, then back to Daniel. "And my parents are still married. She just got a good offer from Penn State, and my dad works here, so it's just temporary."

"And then you guys'll move to Pennsylvania?" Daniel tried to choke back the raw dread in his voice.

Anna lifted her shoulders. "Or they'll move back down here if she finds something closer."

"Or we'll all end up somewhere *else*," Edward said with a laugh. He scooped the mix of veggies and let them fall back in place, a waterfall of bright and healthy colors.

"What about you?" Anna asked. "Have you always lived a few doors down?" She straightened one of the forks and smiled up at Daniel. He couldn't tell if she was playing with him, or if she liked him.

"I was born in Beaufort. We moved into this house when I was eight, so it's all I really remember. My dad pretty much built the entire thing by hand. He was a carpenter. Then my parents divorced a few years ago."

Anna's smile faded.

"It's okay though," Daniel said quickly. "Sometimes I think it's better than staying together and making everyone else miserable with the fighting."

Anna nodded. Edward turned and placed the massive bowl of salad in the center of the table.

"Do you see your dad much?" Anna asked.

Daniel laughed, but obviously with more than humor in his voice. Anna held her palms up and shook her head. "I'm sorry to pry," she said. "You probably think I'm nosy."

The others sat down, and Daniel did the same. He draped a cloth napkin over his lap.

"No, it's okay," he said. "I actually hadn't seen him in over a year until yesterday."

"*Yesterday*?" Anna screwed her face up in confusion. Edward craned out a large scoop of salad and dangled it ponderously in Daniel's direction. Daniel snatched up his plate and held it under the bushy load. Edward released it, and the plate blossomed with leafiness.

"Yeah," he said to Anna. "A guy from the power company dropped him off on our doorstep. He's living in our toolshed."

Daniel grinned at her and basked in her look of disbelief.

"You're not serious."

"As a heart attack," Daniel said.

Edward laughed at that. He got up, grabbed the tomatoes, and added them to the table. Anna poured water from a pitcher into each of the three cups. Daniel looked through the selection of warm dressings for the one with the most fat.

"So, mister . . ." Daniel looked to Edward to fill in the blank. He still didn't know Anna's last name.

"It's Redding," he said, "but I prefer Edward."

"Okay." Daniel swallowed. Even with permission, it felt unnatural to call him by his first name. "What do you do?"

"I'm a chemical engineer," he said. "I work for a plant outside of town. It's terribly boring stuff, I'm afraid."

"It's actually not," Anna told Daniel, stabbing a hunk of tomato. "He breeds and grows micro-organisms that turn regular stuff into useful compounds, kinda like how England once turned chestnuts into acetone."

"Oh, yeah," Daniel said. "Solid reference. Now I know exactly what you're talking about."

Edward laughed. "You kids dig in." He jabbed his salad with an audible crunch.

Daniel took a bite and was pleasantly surprised. The three of them ate amid a chorus of pleasant munching sounds. He forked a tomato and added it to his plate.

After a minute of contented silence, Daniel asked, "Any word on when we'll get power or phones back?"

Edward held up a finger; his mouth was full of a large bite of salad.

"It's just that my brother was away when the storm

hit," Daniel said. "He had my mom's car, and my stepdad's is in the shop, so we can't get word to him."

Edward wiped his beard with his napkin, then returned it to his lap.

"Power might be out for weeks," he said. He nodded toward Anna. "We tried to go out yesterday morning to see what the damage was around town, but couldn't even get out of the neighborhood."

"There was a huge tree down across the entrance," Anna said. "Most of those chainsaws you heard yesterday were probably from the guys working on it."

"We were gonna try and get out this afternoon," Edward said. "I've got a chain and my old Bronco has four wheel drive. I was thinking we could help clear some roads." He lifted his shoulders like he wanted to do more, but clearing roads with a chain was all he could think to contribute. Daniel thought about the charging station outside and wished he was more like these people.

"I could come and help," he said. He lifted his fork with another bite. "And we've got a chainsaw."

Edward nodded. He looked to Anna.

"That'd be awesome," she said.

Daniel thought he noted a bit of a blush on her cheeks as she looked away from him and toward her plate. But it could've been the light reflected off the large hunk of juicy tomato she was steering toward her mouth.

22

After thanking Edward and Anna for the incredible meal and helping scrape the dishes into their compost bucket, Daniel gathered his newly charged devices and headed home. He felt a bounce in his step, even as he powered on the Zune and listened to radio chatter about the worst hurricane since Katrina. They were still talking about the landfall being "near Charleston," which Daniel supposed gave the outside world the best geographical context. He was guilty of doing the same when he was out of town and people asked him where he was from. "Near Charleston," he would say. And that was precisely where hurricane Anna had struck.

He turned up his driveway and looked toward the sound of the buzzing chainsaw, expecting to find Carlton wielding it, but it was his dad. Daniel steered his direction and pulled his ear buds out. He stepped over yet another tree that awaited transmutation into firewood.

His dad cut partway through a log, rolled it over with his shoe, then sliced through the rest. As the stubby cylinder rolled away from the tree, he killed the saw, which came to a rattling stop.

"Back already?" His father set the chainsaw down and pulled a rag from his back pocket. He wiped the sweat from his face and the back of his neck, a gesture that yanked Daniel through the years to a long ago past. He pictured his dad with his shirt off, a tool belt slung low over one hip, a rectangular pencil tucked behind an ear, a ten-penny nail held between pursed and concentrating lips, a hammer wielded like a dexterous extension of his flesh—

Daniel had no idea if his dad had been sober back then, but in his mind he had been capable of anything. He looked past his father to the house he had built with a few friends, a massive tree crashed right through the roof. One dormer was crushed, the other standing. Before, the house had appeared to be winking, now it looked more like it had suffered a blow, like it had a black eye. It had gone from something happy to something that needed stitches.

"Your mom put together some fine sandwiches if you're still hungry," his dad said.

"I filled up on salad, if you can believe that." Daniel patted his stomach. "Is everyone still eating?"

"I think they're working on your sister's room and the living room." He waved his hand at the yard. "This feels productive out here, but it ain't really that necessary. It's just busy work to keep from thinking on all else we can't do."

"Well, the Reddings down the street are gonna take their four by four to see if the roads are clear. I was wondering if we could borrow the chainsaw. They've got a chain and some other stuff to help move trees."

His dad knelt by the chainsaw and opened a black cap. He leaned the machine to the side. "Let me top up the bar oil for you. You should take the gas can as well. Fill 'er up if anyone out there is pumping."

He went to the tall pile of neatly stacked logs and grabbed a green container from the top. A thick, molasses-like oil dripped from it and into the chainsaw. "You know how to crank and use this thing?"

"I'm hoping Edwa—that mister Redding does," Daniel said. "I'm mostly going along 'cause they said we could see if the roads were clear all the way to Hunter's girlfriend's house. I'm thinking they must be blocked in for him not to have come home yet, especially since he knows he has the only car."

His dad put the cap back on the oil canister and tightened the plug on the chainsaw. He stood up and pulled his handkerchief from his back pocket again, wiping his hands on it. "Maybe I should come with you," he said.

Daniel waved his hands. "No. That's okay. I don't want to impose on them—"

"Impose? I'll be coming along to help."

"That's okay, Dad."

"Let's go ask your mom." He picked up the chainsaw and turned toward the house.

"Dad, I really don't want you coming along."

His father threw a hurt look back at him. Daniel immediately felt bad for how it had come out.

"It's just that there's a girl going along, and I really don't want you embarrassing me."

His father smiled. "It's *my* chainsaw. I traded what was left of my boat for it and a ride. So if it's going, *I'm* going." He winked and marched toward the front door.

"Wait," Daniel said. "You traded your *boat* for that saw?"

His dad stopped. "What was left of it," he said.

"And how much was left of it?"

He shrugged. "Not enough to float, probably."

"For a chainsaw," Daniel said.

His dad turned around to face him. "These things are worth their weight in gold after a storm. You've seen that for yourself."

"So you knew mom would let you stay."

"I knew you guys would be in need of one." He looked up at the tree leaning against their house. "Hell, I betcha I could whittle away at that thing if I was roped in and had some help."

"And now you're using it to come along and see Hunter."

His father smiled. "Let's not pose it to your mom quite like that," he said.

With that, he turned and bounded up the steps toward the screen door, while Daniel remained rooted to the sidewalk, the deviousness of his father competing in his brain with the man's generosity. He had a hard time sorting out which motivation had swept him back into their lives. The awful truth was that he preferred to think it was the former, so he could stay comfortable hating his dad. Once a person got used to the feeling, it wasn't so bad. It was all the back and forth that proved exhausting.

****

Daniel remained silent while his father introduced himself to Anna and Edward. A heavy chain was lifted from the garage floor and rattled into a coil in the back of a beat up Ford Bronco. Daniel's father placed the chainsaw beside it, and Daniel added the small red canister, sloshing a quarter-full with fuel. They loaded up, Anna and Daniel sliding into the back seat, the adults up front. Edward pulled out of the garage. An elderly couple crouching by the recharging station turned and waved as they pulled down the driveway. Edward coaxed a friendly beep out of the Bronco's horn.

"Just to warn you guys, it might be a short drive." Edward turned to Daniel's father. "We couldn't even get out of the neighborhood yesterday."

"There's a way," his father said. "If the street's still blocked, I'll show you how we got in along the power lines."

They took a sharp turn at the end of the street, and Daniel reached for the oh-shit handle where it would have been in his mom's car. It wasn't where he expected, so his other hand went to the bench seat to steady himself. It landed on the back of Anna's hand, which retreated as if bit.

"Sorry," Daniel whispered. He wiggled in his seat to demonstrate a new level of commitment to keeping his balance.

"It's okay," Anna said, folding her hands in her lap. The two of them gazed out their windows and enjoyed the breeze as the Bronco rumbled through the neighborhood.

"There's a bad one up here," Edward said. He pointed over the dash and slowed down as they passed a house that had lost half its roof. Globs of pink insulation hung in the trees like cotton candy. Rafters stuck out like ribs over a gaping void, like God had been in the middle of a heart transplant when he got called away.

"We talked to the owners yesterday," Anna said. "They're staying with neighbors. Their story of the night of the storm was horrific."

"I bet," Daniel said. He met his father's gaze in the side view mirror. Something in his dad's frown suggested that his own survival story would be hard to match.

"Looks like they got that tree parted."

Daniel and Anna both leaned toward the middle of the seat so they could peer through the windshield. Ahead, Daniel could see that it was one of the ancient oaks framing the neighborhood's entrance that had fallen across the road. To the left, the head of the tree lay in a crumbled heap, the long arms of the great oak broken and twisted and sprouting bushy plumes of leaves up toward the sky in every direction. On the other side of the drive, a round disk of thick soil had levered up to vertical with the ripping of the roots. A clod of mud with tendrils poking out of it formed a massive wall at the base of the tree. The tufts of grass clinging to the other side were still green and seemingly oblivious to their topsy-turvy fate.

Daniel whistled at the sight of the fallen monster. It had fallen parallel to the main road, right across the entrance to the neighborhood, and had to be six or more feet thick. With the deep drainage ditch beyond, it had once been an impassible barrier. But now it was cut. Edward steered for the gap in the tree where a chunk not quite a lane wide had been removed. Daniel wondered just what kind of saw had been able to chew through the thing. He felt his shoulder brush up against Anna's and tried not to pull away without it seeming like he was lingering on purpose. Any extra pressure might be seen as flirting, and too forward. Anything less would be intolerable to him.

As the Bronco crept through the gap in the tree, Anna leaned toward her window and Daniel reluctantly did the same, there no longer being an excuse to linger in the middle. He watched the yellow wall of concentric circles pass close by, the smell of fresh wood pervading the car. There were jagged splinters standing out near the center where the weight of the cut piece had ripped as it was pulled out. The bite marks of several angles of attack from various saws met in rough ridges. As they pulled out the other side, Daniel saw the removed piece was actually several. They had been drug away, leaving a smear of bark in their wake. A car passed along in front of the Bronco, creeping down the main road at half the speed limit, a bank of shocked faces turning to gape at the fortress wall lowered over the neighborhood's entrance and now cut clean through.

"We should stop and take pictures," Anna said. She leaned out her window and aimed a small camera back at the tree. It made fake shutter sounds.

"On the way back," Edward said. He turned to Daniel. "Which way?"

"Right," Daniel said. He repeated the directions his mom had given him. "Down 105 for a few miles, then right on Harvey. The neighborhood's called Willow Falls. Second house on the left."

Edward nodded and hit his blinker. They turned slowly and headed down the highway. Several times a mile, each of them would take turns pointing to another scene of destruction: a large tree pushed off the road, a power line down and tangled up in the tree that took it, a snapped power pole, a mobile home that had been lifted up from its foundation and set back down roughly in the front yard, its walls canting to the side.

"Look at that barn," Daniel said. He pointed to the old wooden structure, its red paint chipping; it was leaning over to one side and completely ruined.

Anna laughed. "It was already like that."

"Oh." Daniel remembered. "You're right."

She slapped him playfully on the arm, and both men up front laughed.

"This is a lot more clear than when I came through," Daniel's father said. "We actually stopped and cut that tree." He pointed. "It was one of the ones we couldn't drive around."

The first stoplight they came to hung still and lifeless. Daniel was surprised to see it hanging at all. Edward slowed to a stop, waited for another vehicle to move funeral-slow through the intersection, then pulled across. Daniel tapped Anna on the shoulder and pointed down the road to where two power trucks were parked, both of their booms tucked down tight.

"Are they doing anything?" she asked, leaning closer to get a good look.

"Doesn't look like it." As far as he could tell, they were just taking notes. He could see an entire line of power poles leaning over into the woods, like the toppling of one had drug the rest down with it. "How do they know where to even begin?" he asked.

"My friend with the company said they'd be getting a ton of out-of-state help," Daniel's father said.

"I imagine most of that help will be routed to Columbia and Charleston," Edward pointed out. He pulled into the other lane to go around a large limb, then came to a stop on the other side of it. "Even if we were hit the hardest, there's probably more damage in dollar values and in terms of population elsewhere." He turned toward the back seat. "You kids wanna haul that limb out of the road?"

Daniel and Anna popped their doors and hurried out. They smiled at each other as they hoisted the large piece of timber and staggered toward the shoulder with it.

"On three," Anna said.

They counted together and tossed it to the side. Daniel rubbed his palms as it tumbled into the ditch.

They hopped back in the Bronco, and Edward put it in gear. As they trundled along, a drive that might've taken fifteen minutes any other time was stretched into over an hour. Daniel and Anna jumped out anytime there was debris to move. The chainsaw was used twice to cut down trees leaning out over the road that looked like they could go at any time. These were cut into smaller pieces and hauled into the ditch. Daniel waved at a man in a pickup who drove by while they were working. Being seen out on the road, volunteering his time to pick up after the storm, filled Daniel's heart with a slightly selfish pride. He couldn't believe how much fun he was having moving trees around. And when his father asked if he wanted to cut the second tree into logs, an appraising glance from Anna made it impossible to refuse. He listened to his dad's instructions, cranked the thing on the first try, then chewed slowly and hesitantly through the middle of a tree as thick as his thigh. He enjoyed the vibration and the shower of yellow snow kicked up from the tool. After the saw dipped through the end of the tree and the upper half sank to the road, he hit the power switch and handed it back to his dad. The smile on his father's face as he took the chainsaw remained fresh in Daniel's mind as he helped Anna and Edward drag away the upper half of the tree he'd just bisected.

It was strange how normal it all felt. Driving along a road with the barest of traffic, working to clear it of debris, listening to his father and Edward exchange small talk, tapping Anna on the arm to point out something, laughing at a joke someone made, taking sober instructions from his father—it was all such a bizarre transition for Daniel that he nearly forgot where they were going, that they were primarily out to find his brother. And that his brother would have no idea Daniel was coming, or who he'd be bringing with him.

22

"There it is," Daniel said, pointing to the "Willow Falls" sign on the side of the road. It was an old wooden sign and partially obscured by a fallen tree. Edward turned the Bronco onto a dirt road wide enough for a single vehicle. The ground to either side was rough with weeds and looked to be mostly sand and crushed shell, the kind of ground that reminded Daniel they weren't far from the ocean. Edward piloted them down the lane, dodging a limb or two. Mailboxes highlighted the occasional driveway, but the neighborhood was even more heavily wooded than Daniel's. The houses were set back far enough to be invisible from the road. To either side, though, Daniel could see the effects of the storm. Jagged spikes of timber stood up everywhere, the tops of the trees angling down like they were taking a bow. Fallen limbs formed an odd sort of underbrush. A smattering of trash could be seen along the banks, likely ripped from a garbage can or scattered by scavengers.

"That's the second one," Daniel's father said, pointing.

Edward slowed and turned onto the gravel drive. The tires crunched along, the smell of salt in the air through the open windows. "We're gonna need the saw," Edward said, rubbing his beard. Daniel and Anna leaned into one another and peered ahead. Two large trees crisscrossed the driveway ahead, their limbs throwing up a hedge of green.

They stopped the car, and Daniel's dad let Daniel make the first cuts. The trunks of the trees were held off the ground by their limbs, which made cutting all the way through them easy. Daniel had less fear of the tool this second time. He pushed the blade deep against the trunk, letting the spiked collar on the chainsaw hold fast, giving him something to pivot against. He let the chain do the work and stood back as the two halves parted. Another smooth cut through the tree, and two through the other one, and Daniel shut the chainsaw down. He handed it and the plastic goggles back to his father.

"Nice work, Son," his dad said. He slapped him on the back. The newness of that trite and clichéd moment—learning a skill from his father and putting it on display—made Daniel feel slightly dizzy and more than a little resentful. He found himself smiling, against his will, and saw that Anna was smiling back at him.

The four of them drug the two trees out of the road, the limbs sweeping the gravel behind them. Back in the Bronco, they trundled along, heading for a house partially visible at the end of the long and wood-lined alley.

"Good golly," Edward said, as they exited into a clearing at the end of the drive.

"Holy shit," Daniel's father said.

Daniel leaned his head out the window to see. The Bronco came to a crunching stop, the brakes squealing. He followed his father's pointing arm to see his mom's Taurus parked in what must've once been a shady spot.

The tree that had formerly created said shade was lying on top of the Taurus, the vehicle now flat from hood to trunk.

"Holy shit," Daniel whispered.

He felt Anna leaning across him, her hand on his shoulder, straining to see. Daniel would've delayed the moment had he been thinking clearly. Instead, he opened the door and stepped out, allowing Anna to spill out behind him.

"Mom's gonna flip," he said. He walked out toward the car, then turned as a screen door slammed by the house.

"Daniel?"

His brother stomped down the wooden steps leading up to the single-story house. He broke into a trot, hurrying his way, his face a mix of surprise, relief, and joy.

"Oh my god," he said, throwing his arms around a stunned Daniel, who just stood there. "My little brother," he said, his hand on the back of Daniel's head, his other hand slapping his back.

"You okay?" Daniel asked. His brother let him go, and Daniel saw a young-looking girl standing on the back deck of the house, a hand on her hip and another shielding her eyes.

"We were gonna set out in the morning on foot if nobody came by," Hunter said. He turned to the Bronco and waved at Anna. Edward was walking around the car, his hand brushing along the hood. The passenger door clicked open—

"No fucking way," Hunter said.

He took a step back toward the crushed Taurus, shaking his head.

"No way."

"He's only staying for a little—" Daniel started.

"Hello, Son," their father said. He took a step toward Hunter, who took another step back. Daniel watched Anna's eyes dart between the two of them, a frown on her face. Suddenly, Daniel felt the embarrassment of his family's dysfunctional nature. He wanted everything to be okay, and fast, even if just for appearances.

"What are you doing here?" Hunter asked.

"Hunter, this is Anna." Daniel waved her direction. "That's her father, Edward. They were kind enough to bring us over."

Hunter waved him off. His eyes hadn't left their father, who at last remained still, a dozen paces from the two of them.

"Do you want to introduce us?" Daniel pointed toward the house.

"That's Chen," he said, his eyes not wavering. "Chen, this is my little brother Daniel and my asshole of a father that I've told you about."

Chen waved tentatively.

"Is it just you two?" Edward asked. He walked toward the Taurus, scratching his beard.

Hunter nodded. As Daniel had suspected, his brother had lied about Chen's parents being home.

"Maybe we can have a moment alone?" their father asked. He pointed down the driveway.

Hunter grunted. He looked around to Chen, who was hugging herself on the back porch and biting her lip. He looked back to his father and nodded. "After you," he said, waving him down the driveway. He refused to budge until their father had already started shuffling away.

"Chen, why don't you see if they need anything to drink?" Hunter called over his shoulder.

Daniel's eyes hardly left his brother during the several exchanges. Somehow, Hunter seemed so much older than Daniel thought of him being. He seemed like their father's peer, the kind of man that played host to other people and owned a house and had a wife and that sort of thing. As his father and older brother walked away, back down the narrow and heavily wooded driveway, Daniel felt Anna tugging him toward the house. He let out his held breath, managed to suck a deep new lungful, and reluctantly followed her.

****

"Hunter talks about you a lot," Chen said. She poured water from a gallon jug like the kind you buy at the grocery store for a buck. She handed Daniel the cup. Anna cradled hers, and Chen began filling another for Edward, who told her to pour half as much for him.

"What does he say?" Daniel laughed and heard the nerves in his voice. Everyone had become uncomfortably quiet after the scene outside.

"Mostly good stuff." Chen smiled, her dark eyes shining. She turned and slid some papers off the kitchen counter. "We managed to get into the glove box through the broken window. Hunter was dying to know if the insurance was up to date." She handed a card to Daniel. Anna finished taking a sip of her water and leaned over to look. "He said he couldn't rest until he knew. Our phone's been dead, and the driveway was blocked even if the car'd been okay. You should've heard it when it hit." Chen shook her head. Her hand was trembling as she poured herself a cup of water.

"It's just good nobody was hurt," Edward said. He looked around the kitchen and out the back door. The tall grasses of marshland could be seen beyond, an old wooden dock slicing out over them. "No major damage to the house?"

"No." Chen took a sip of water. "We were real lucky. My parents, though, were in Columbia, so they have to be worried sick. Do any of your phones work?"

They all shook their heads.

"Columbia got hit pretty hard, too," Daniel said. "Lots of tornados spun off, according to the radio."

Chen laughed. "The only radio we had was the car's. We actually managed to squeeze in and turn it on, but the battery didn't last and the antenna must've been messed up. We heard mostly static."

"You've had plenty of food and water?" Daniel asked.

Chen nodded. "We've been heating stuff up on the grill outside. The cover got sucked off it, but everything else is fine. We were actually going to try and walk to your house today, or at least until someone gave us a ride, but decided to wait one more day to see if the phones came back."

"The phones are going to be out for a while," Edward said. "But we'll give you a ride out of here. Why don't you gather some things together and maybe write a note to your parents just in case."

"Yeah," Chen said. "Okay." She smiled at them and headed down a hallway off the kitchen. "You guys just make yourselves at home," she called out. "I'll just grab a few things and be right back."

****

Daniel peered out the living room window at the demolished Taurus, past the Bronco, and down the shaded driveway. He thought he saw movement out there, but couldn't be sure. He was glad the conversation was taking place somewhere private, but he was dying to know what was being said.

"You okay?" Anna asked. She walked out to join him by the window.

Daniel turned and smiled. "I'm fine. Sorry to drag you guys into my family crap."

"Are you kidding?" Anna stepped beside him and peered out at what was left of the Taurus. "Somebody needed to come out here. That would've been a long walk back to your house."

Daniel watched her lean forward, cup her hands around her face, and press the sides of her palms against the window to peer out. The back of her neck, the faint whiff of her presence, so much about this girl he had spent all of a few hours around seemed so intimately familiar. He wondered if he was going crazy, if he was insanely desperate to be with someone, if the storm had triggered some sort of apocalyptic, end-of-the-world, one-last-time, one-*first*-time, procreation urge. Wasn't any of that infinitely more likely than love at first sight? Did people even believe in that bullshit anymore?

"Whatcha thinking?" Anna asked.

Daniel's brain whizzed back to reality from wherever it had gone. He saw that Anna was looking at him, and that he had been staring at her. He was pretty sure he looked like a creeper in that moment, the sort of blank stare from hyper-concentration (or complete lack thereof) that made him vastly unpopular.

"Nothing," he lied, looking away. "I just spaced out there for a second. Tired, I guess."

Chen paced though the kitchen and joined them in the living room. "I'm almost ready," she said. She set a black suitcase down by the door. "Just need to write a note and grab some food that might spoil."

"I'll help with the food," Anna said. She reached over and squeezed Daniel's hand for the barest of moments, then turned and followed Chen to the kitchen. Daniel's hand leapt up in some delayed response. He looked at his palm and wondered what had just happened.

Had it happened? What did it mean? Just a friendly gesture, right? Commiserating with his family stuff. Understanding him, what with her parents living apart. Or had he found someone as crazy as himself living just four houses down?

Outside, Edward walked by, having circled the house. He seemed to be surveying the roof and the siding for damage. Beyond him, Daniel could see his brother marching up the driveway, his arms stiff, unswinging and powerful before him, hands balled into fists. He wore an adult scowl and moved with purpose. Daniel grabbed the black suitcase, pushed the screen door open, and hurried toward the Bronco.

"Chen's inside?" Hunter asked, meeting Daniel by the Bronco.

"Yeah. She's rounding up some food, I think."

Hunter pointed to the suitcase, which Daniel loaded into the rear bed of the Bronco. "That hers?"

"Yeah."

"So I guess we're going with you guys?"

Daniel turned and nodded toward the Taurus. "Were you gonna stay here? She said you guys were gonna start walking tomorrow anyway."

Hunter shook his head. He ran his hand up over his forehead and through his hair. "Why'd you bring him here?" he asked. "Why would Mom let him stay?"

"He traded his boat for a chainsaw," Daniel said, wishing he could make his brother understand—even though he knew it was all a lot more complicated than it seemed in his head. "Did he tell you he quit drinking?"

"Yeah," Hunter said. "He also told me that seven years ago and a hundred times since."

"I think he's changed," Daniel said.

A brief flash of rage spun across Hunter's face before he managed to look away.

"You always think he's changed," he said.

Daniel wanted to plead more, not for a strong belief in his father, which he didn't feel, but to soothe his brother. He wanted to keep lying to make things better, but he knew it would make them worse.

Hunter laughed. "He really sleeping in the toolshed?" he asked.

"Yeah," Daniel said. "I thought Mom was joking, but she lets the chainsaw stay in the house while he sleeps in the shed."

"That's pretty funny." Hunter turned and smiled at Daniel. "Damn, dude, I'm glad you're okay. How's Zola?"

"She's fine. Her thumbs don't know what to do with the cell towers out. She misses her friends, and a tree went through her bed and ruined a ton of her shit, but she seems to actually be fine."

"This is pretty fucked up," Hunter said, looking around at all the trees and scattered branches. Daniel noticed not a piece of the debris had been moved. There were no piles of branches like around his neighborhood. He imagined Hunter and Chen had been rolling around in bed doing whatever couples did while he'd been working his ass off and worried about them.

"We should totally be in school right now," Daniel said.

They turned to the sound of the screen door snapping shut. Chen and Anna came out, plastic grocery bags in either hand. Edward headed toward the Bronco from the far corner of the house.

"You got all your things?" Daniel asked his brother.

He patted his pockets. "Heh. I just checked to see if I had the keys to the car. Yeah, I've got my wallet and phone."

"I packed your other clothes in the suitcase," Chen said. Daniel took bags of food and a gallon of water from her and put them in the back of the Bronco. Anna unloaded her arms as well, then began rearranging the stuff in the back, pressing it all to the sides, leaving room in the middle.

"I guess we'll be sitting back here," she said, referring to the cargo compartment behind the rear seat.

Daniel nodded. He watched his father make his sullen way up the drive, hands in his pockets, chin down, feet dragging. He looked like a whipped dog, and Daniel no longer wanted to know what had been said between them. He didn't want to feel any sorrier for his dad than he already did.

As Hunter and Chen got in the back seat and his father and Edward slid in up front, Daniel felt overwhelmed with how *right* the pairing felt. The presence of another couple seemed to solidify something between him and Anna—some vicarious romantic energy. *We are what they are.* He and Anna crawled in the back amid the bags of food and the suitcase. Daniel grabbed the top edge of the hinged rear door, its window down, and swung it shut. It banged and latched with the raw metal sound of an older car, and they were off, crunching the gravel driveway, turning their back on the empty house and ruined family car, working their way down the narrow alley of wounded and broken trees, the glare of the sun dimming as they passed through the mottled shade, then out to the unbroken shine and steady thrum of civilized pavement beyond.

23

The world went by in reverse. Daniel and Anna watched the past from the back of the Bronco, the road sliding off into the distance as they leaned against the back of the seat and peered out the rear window. A tree that they had cut and hauled out of the way just hours before popped into view and then slid away from them. The plastic grocery bags rustled in the breeze. Bits of conversation from the two men in the front drifted back, but in an indistinguishable slur. The deep silence from Hunter and Chen was much nearer.

Daniel felt his body unwind from the several days of tension. He relaxed against the seat behind him and felt the raw terror of his life—not the storm aftermath, but of his normal life—slide out his pores. He felt happy and calm in a way he couldn't remember since childhood. Maybe it was knowing his brother was okay, that his entire family was okay. Perhaps it was the chilly breeze passing through the car, cooling the sweat on the back of his neck, making his hair dance on his scalp. Maybe it was the thrill of being one of the only vehicles in sight, or the view of all the destruction sliding over the horizon, reminding him how awesome it was to be alive. He soaked in the unusual state of bliss. He felt his shoulder bump up against Anna's as the Bronco lurched to the side. He felt Anna press herself closer, so that the contact between them *remained* long after the limb Edward had dodged disappeared into the past.

Maybe it was all the emotional outpouring of the last few days, the thrill of the unknowable future rushing at him blindly from behind, not knowing when he'd go to school again, not knowing when he'd watch TV again, not knowing when his cell phone would come back to life and continue its unringing mocking. It could have been any or all of these things that caused him to do the unthinkable, the laughable, the it-only-happens-in-the-movies:

He reached over and grabbed Anna's hand.

It was so easy. It was like he couldn't *not* do it. He felt her warm and soft palm against his own, felt her small and dexterous fingers curl around his, *accepting*. He rubbed his thumb up and down the back of her fingers, marveling at how simple and correct the harmless act felt. Some kind of raw power surged through him, a joy that threatened to burst out through his chest if his heart couldn't contain it. Then Anna tilted her head to the side and rested it on Daniel's shoulder, and she made the unimprovable *better*.

The world slid into the past. The future came at them blindly. With the wind drowning out the sound of the blinker, the stops and turns took them by surprise, causing them to stiffen and brace for what came next. But they remained like that, leaning on one another, hands caressing hands, fingers learning how they interlocked, and Daniel realized that if it was happening so fast, it wasn't because of anything apocalyptic. He realized that Anna had been waiting just as long for him as he had been for her.

24

As they rode slowly through town, Daniel was glad for the extended tour and the leisurely pace. He could've ridden in that Bronco forever.

They passed a gas station with a line of vehicles all trying to get to a single pump. The rattle of a portable generator and the sight of a man in coveralls working the nozzle gave them a bit of hope that civilization could reopen for business, albeit slowly and at a trickle.

Two police cars sat outside the Save-Mart, their blue lights flashing in circles. There was yellow tape over the front glass, which was patched with full sheets of plywood.

"Storm damage or looting?" Daniel asked.

Anna let go of his hand to grab the edge of the rear window and peer out. "I hope storm damage," she said, but not too convincingly.

Daniel rubbed his hands together. He felt the residual heat from her skin touching his. He glanced at Anna's hand and had the powerful surety that he could grab it again if he wanted. It was a new power, like waking up one morning to discover you could fly. He could touch someone in a loving way and have them not flinch, or think him a creep. They would even reciprocate.

Daniel had a sudden impulse to leap out of the back of the Bronco and run down the street, screaming at the top of his voice.

"Look at that," Anna said. She pointed off to the other side. Daniel could hear his father and Edward jabbering in the front. His brother cursed.

Daniel leaned forward and peered out the back of the Bronco and off to the side. The hulk of a dozen boats were scattered over the marsh between the highway and the Beaufort River. Normally, the craft were bobbing in the gentle swell or stiff current of the ever-changing tide, like ducks all swimming in the same direction. The high tide and storm surge had pulled their moorings free and had dragged them over dry land before receding. Now they sat on their sides, forlorn and looking like toys, masts angling up toward the sky in unusual angles, the tatters of an unfurled headsail hanging from a forestay like laundry left out to dry. A pickup truck was parked out on a gravel turnout, the driver standing by the front bumper, his hands on the sides of his head, elbows jutting, disbelieving, to either side. Daniel wondered if he was one of the owners, or just a stunned gawker like the rest of them.

"Over there," Anna said.

She pointed across the river. Daniel saw the stern and prop of a boat lost among the trees on the far bank. A small sailboat stood high and dry, tangled in the broken limbs of an old oak. It seemed to be what Anna was pointing at. He heard Hunter and Chen conversing back and forth; he looked to the side to see their faces hanging out the window, eyes wide and darting.

Daniel imagined what the City Marina must look like if this anchorage, known affectionately as "Hurricane

Hole" for its relatively nice protection, could be so decimated. He was frankly glad when Edward did a U-Turn at the end of town and started heading back toward home, keeping him from having to see what his dad had been through.

"Doesn't look like much of anything's open for business," Daniel said.

They passed the gas station with the single operational pump. Edward didn't even slow down, obviously deciding he had enough fuel to not endure the wait.

"It's only been two days," Anna pointed out. Daniel felt a stabbing fear that she was referring to their hand-holding and the rapidity of his feelings for her. He shook such doubts away. She was talking about the storm, the signs of progress already. She was saying that this was as bad as it would be, and it would only get better.

Daniel nearly reached out and tested whatever was between them by grabbing her hand, but such actions still felt like they needed a *moment*. It could feel casual and right during a *moment*, but not just anytime. Right then, it would have felt desperate. Physical, rather than emotional. Daniel marveled that he knew such things. He could now see through walls as well as fly. He wondered what other new powers he'd discover next.

The Bronco picked up speed as they left town, and Daniel and Anna watched the road move beneath them, their chins hanging over the rear door. Sporadic traffic roared by in the other direction. Daniel waved to some kids in the back of a pickup, who waved back.

They turned into their neighborhood, and Hunter whistled at the sight of the tree across the road. Edward steered them through the tight gap once again, the smell of cut wood and sap just as strong as before. Chainsaws were still busy at work somewhere. People were out doing what Daniel had been doing for days: dragging limbs, waving to foreign neighbors, drinking warm water and sweating. He felt like an explorer returning home from a dangerous circumnavigation. He felt alive with a new knowledge of what the outside world looked like and what other people were going through. He imagined himself going door to door to fill people in, despite the fact that they could just as easily drive through town and gawk for themselves.

Edward passed by his and Anna's house and drove to the end of the cul-de-sac. He pulled up Daniel's driveway, past the several neat mounds of debris.

"Holy shit," Hunter said, when he saw the size of the tree resting against the house.

Chen said something to him about watching his language as the Bronco squealed to a stop. Doors popped open and the six of them staggered out.

Daniel heard Zola squeal their mother's name. She then ran across the yard and threw herself into Hunter's arms, who picked her up and spun her around. For Daniel, the scene was as bizarre and new as the tree denting their roof. Their mom walked briskly across the yard, tugging her gloves off, and waited for Zola to be set down. She hugged Hunter, her eyes wet with tears. She let go and stepped back to look at him, her hands still on his cheeks.

"You okay?" she asked.

Hunter looked embarrassed. "I'm fine."

Their mother nodded to Chen, then reached out and hugged her. She glanced at Daniel over Chen's shoulder, then her eyes went to Anna and widened.

"Mom, this is Anna."

He wanted to add *my girlfriend, whose hand I've held*, but refrained.

"Nice to meet you," she said, letting go of Chen and shaking her hand.

"And this is her dad, Edward." His mom turned and waved, thanking him. Edward smiled back, and Daniel saw the way their father was watching the entire scene from across the hood of the Bronco. His mother looked at their father for a second, and his father smiled. Daniel could've sworn his mom nodded his direction just a little as she squeezed Hunter's arm.

"Carlton borrowed a canister of propane from the couple across the street," their mom said. "He's grilling some chicken out back before it spoils. Daniel, why don't you go see if he needs any help." She nodded to Hunter and Chen. "You two can get freshened up. And Edward, we've got plenty if the two of you will join us. It's the least we can do to repay you for picking Hunter up."

"Love to," Edward said, smiling. He rubbed his beard. "Let's unload and I'll go park the car and grab some tomatoes."

"Yum," Hunter said, rubbing his stomach.

Daniel wanted to point out to his mom that Hunter and Chen hadn't been doing much of anything for the past two days and didn't need "freshening up." But Anna was grabbing bags out of the back and forcing them into his hands, his mother shooing him toward the house before he could complain. Before he knew it, he was setting the bags down in the dining room and watching the Bronco back out of the driveway. He could see Anna's face in the passenger seat as she peered out toward the house. Daniel wondered suddenly if the connection between them would be severed as soon as she was out of sight. What would it feel like to see her again, for the first time post-hand-holding? What *were* they? How did millions of people go through this and survive to giggle about it on the other side?

Daniel pulled some canned goods from one of the bags and arranged them on the table. He could feel a powerful depression looming if Anna decided their *moment* had been a mistake. It was easy to imagine only Edward coming over for dinner, telling the rest of them that "Anna didn't feel well," casting a glance toward Daniel as if he'd done something wrong.

Misery and joy, Daniel decided. *This is how you know you're in love.*

25

Fortunately, Anna did come over, and a shy smile in Daniel's direction let him know their bond could survive stretching the length of their neighborhood. She and her dad arranged some vegetables on the chopping block in the kitchen. Everyone else was out back, wrestling the furniture on the rear deck into place, picking the twigs and leaves out of the webbed chairs and fussing over the smorgasbord of food scavenged from the cabinets. Daniel could see Carlton and his dad standing by the grill, the chicken hissing and smoking, two small pots on the upper rack spitting with side dishes. The sight of the two men—father and stepfather—standing together amicably seemed surreal. Daniel accepted the plate of freshly sliced tomatoes shoved into his hands and allowed Anna to steer him toward the sliding screen door.

"I think we're almost ready," his mom yelled at the upper floor. Daniel heard his brother shout something back through the open window. The temporary sleeping arrangements had been quickly set: Daniel was moving into Hunter's room with his brother, and Chen and Zola were sharing his. He had tried not to grumble about it too much. His brother had looked ready to be dropped back off at Chen's house.

"Grab a plate," his mom said. She pointed to a stack of paper plates on the table. Daniel grabbed one for Anna and took one for himself. Carlton dropped a piece of BBQ-rubbed chicken on each of their plates. Daniel's father added a scoop of warmed-up canned beans and instant mashed potatoes. To Daniel, the sparse fare looked like Thanksgiving.

His brother and Chen joined them on the deck, followed soon after by Zola. Edward went around forking slices of tomato onto everyone's plates. Daniel and Anna sat on the steps leading down to the back yard while the others scrambled for room around the oval table. Their father put his food together last and ate standing, his cup balanced on the deck's wooden rail.

While they ate, Hunter and Edward took turns telling the others about what they'd seen in town, about the gas pump, the cops at the grocery store, the beached fleet of sailboats, all the downed power lines and the wrecked roofs. Zola asked if there'd been any cell phone signal, and everyone was surprised to realize that they hadn't even checked.

Daniel dove into his food and watched Anna enjoy hers. They exchanged smiles while they chewed, as if the two of them possessed a secret. Chainsaws hummed in the distance; everyone laughed and ate and gossiped. Chen seemed to take perverse delight in telling their mom that she'd warned Hunter to park the Taurus out in the yard. News of the car, however, was still a sore spot for their mom, who chewed her dinner and didn't laugh with the others while they recounted their search for the insurance card and their attempts to work the radio.

As far as Daniel could tell, it was the most normal, bizarre meal he'd ever had. Looking up, he could see the limbs of the great oak from the front yard reaching over the peak of the damaged roof. One massive broken limb draped over the back and was bushy with leaves. That he could get so quickly used to such newness as the tree on his house made his infatuation with Anna almost believable. Which was stranger or more sudden? As Anna stabbed the last of his tomato off his plate and popped it into her mouth, Daniel slashed at her fork with his as if jousting, and oddly enough wished that nothing in his world would ever change—

"Holy shit, I've got a bar," Zola said.

"Language, young lady," their mother said, but everyone else stopped chewing and turned to look at her. She held her phone in the air, tilted the screen down and peered up at it. She spun in place, as if trying to divine the pocket of most reception. Hunter and Chen both began digging their phones out of their pockets.

"It's gone," Zola said. She walked down the steps between Daniel and Anna, waving the phone in the air. "Come back," she called after the ephemeral bar.

"I've got signal," Hunter said. He pressed some buttons.

"Who're you calling?" Chen asked.

"You," he said. Everyone sat breathless. He lowered the phone and looked at it. "It says the network is full."

"Me too," Zola said, holding the phone to her ear.

"I bet everyone is trying to use them," Daniel pointed out.

"There might be signal but no service for quite some time," Edward said.

"Honey, don't just keep redialing." Their mother

snapped her fingers in Zola's direction. "Just try once an hour. Don't waste your battery."

Anna seemed like she was going to say something about the batteries—maybe remind them of her charging station—but chose not to.

"Let's not get all worked up," their father said. "These things will come back in time, but trying to rush them won't make it happen any faster." He gathered plates from the table and stacked them together. Daniel watched his mom as she studied his actions. She handed her own empty plate to him, her eyes darting from him to Carlton.

"Thanks for cooking," their father said, nodding to Carlton. "I'm going to get out of ya'lls hair for a while. Tomorrow, though, I'm gonna want to borrow that saw." He turned and looked to Edward, who seemed to have bonded with their father during the day's ride. "If you don't mind, I'd like to head over and get that rope we talked about, so I'll have it in the morning."

"What're you gonna do in the morning?" Daniel asked.

"*We*," his father said. He glanced up. "We're gonna get that tree off this house I built. We're not gonna wait around for someone else to come and do it for us."

His father gave him a most sober stare. He stepped between Daniel and Anna and strolled purposefully toward Edward's house.

Edward thanked Carlton and his mom for their hospitality and hurried off as well. Daniel's mom stood still, an empty plate in her hand. She looked up at the broken bough of the massive tree hanging over the top of the roof.

"I guess I'd better go," Anna told Daniel, the lilt of her voice seeming to complain at having to do so. She stood up and brushed the back of her shorts with her hands. Daniel stood as well and took her plate, stacking it under his own.

"Maybe I should come over and help Dad carry whatever he's borrowing." He knew it was a transparent excuse to stay near her, but he didn't care. If he could be so bold in the back of the Bronco, he could let someone know he'd rather not see them go.

Anna smiled. She bit her lip and nodded. Daniel threw the plates in a trash bag Hunter was using to gather dishes. He mumbled to his mom that he'd be right back, then chased Anna off the deck and around the house toward the street.

****

"That was an amazing meal," Daniel said, making small talk while they walked the short trip between their houses.

"Yeah." Anna turned her head to follow the flight of a startled blue jay. "Your brother seems like a cool guy. And your sister's sweet."

Daniel refrained from arguing the points. "Do you miss your brother?" he asked.

Anna nodded. She kicked a small limb off the street. "A lot. It was cool for a while to have the house to myself, but now it's just boring."

"How do you like being home schooled? And why did your parents choose to do that?"

"They didn't. I did." Anna tucked her hands into her back pocket. She veered to the side and nudged Daniel with her shoulder. "After middle school, I told them I was either gonna home school or just drop out and wait until I could take my GED. I couldn't handle it."

"Couldn't handle what?"

She looked away. "Just stuff. Girls. Meanness." She tried to smile at Daniel, but her eyes were shining wet. "I was always sort of this tomgirl. I enjoyed tinkering with my dad in the garage. I liked playing whatever my brother was playing. I mean, I loved my mom and all, but she was always the one working long hours and away on business. There was a lot of role reversal in my house, and it didn't match what my peers were going through."

"You and I have a lot in common, then," Daniel said. "Girls have a long history of being mean to me as well." He laughed, hoping she'd take the admission as a joke.

"Maybe they hate us for being cooler than them," Anna offered.

"I'm sure that's it."

They stopped in front of Anna's driveway and looked up at the house. Daniel nearly asked her if she wanted to keep walking some more, maybe to Georgia and back, but her father waved from the open garage, so they trudged up toward the house.

Daniel's dad was coiling a long length of rope when they joined them. Another neat loop of rope lay at his feet. "You don't have any webbing by any chance, do you?" he asked Anna's father.

"I've got these tow straps," he said, digging them out of a box and holding them up.

"Perfect."

"I came over to see if you needed help carrying this stuff back," Daniel said.

His father flashed him a knowing smile, his eyes darting happily between him and Anna.

"Hey," Anna said, "I never showed you how that water flows down to our sink."

"Oh, yeah, I meant to ask you about that."

"Hey Dad, I'm gonna take Daniel up to see our cistern."

Edward laughed and worked to unknot lengths of flat yellow webbing. "Go right ahead," he said.

"I'll wait for you," his father said, "so don't be too long."

Daniel waved and followed Anna into the house. She checked over her shoulder with a smile before turning a corner and padding up the stairs. Daniel hurried after her.

At the top of the stairs, she rounded a banister, her hand squeaking on the wood, and paced toward one of the bedrooms. She stood outside the door, looking in and waiting for Daniel.

"We were filling up the bathtubs before the storm," she said. "Dad and I were trying to think of ways to store up even more."

Daniel joined her and looked inside. There was a kiddie pool in the middle of the bedroom, sitting on top of a bed frame and box spring. The mattress was leaning on its side against a wall, out of the way.

"What in the world?" Daniel asked.

"Come look." Anna walked around the pool to the bedroom window. She stuck a finger against the glass, pointing to a hose outside. "We set it up in a hurry, but it works great. Once we got the pool up here, Dad reached out the window and popped the downspout off the gutter. He held me while I taped that hose to where the downspout was."

Daniel looked up through the window to see a length of garden hose duct-taped to the short drop of spout leading off the gutter. The hose came through the top part of the window, which was cracked open, and led to the pool.

"Mom would've killed us," Anna said. She laughed.

"So the water flows from the gutter into the pool," Daniel said. He looked back at the pool, which was half full. "Why didn't it overflow? There was tons of rain with that storm."

"It did overflow," Anna said. She pointed to a hose trailing off the upper lip of the pool, gobs of caulk rimming a small indention that had been cut into the plastic. The hose snaked straight from the elevated lip of the pool and out the bottom of the window. "See? The pool overflowed into the sink all night, where the excess went down the drain and back outside. We let the gutters run clean first, then started collecting as much as we could."

"This hose looks like it goes up a little." Daniel ran his hand along the length of green hose, checking the angle.

Anna nodded. "As long as you don't let any air in, it'll keep siphoning off. The carpet did get a little wet from the house shaking so much when the wind blew. Water was sloshing everywhere, and we'd designed it to keep the pool full. Next time, I'd probably set the overflow hose a little lower."

Daniel looked the contraption over. Along with the charging station outside, it was like Anna and her Father were a Rube Goldberg factory. "Do you get extra credit for any of this stuff?"

Anna laughed. "I wish. Unfortunately, it's all standardized testing for memorized crap you could just look up if you needed to. My dad and I just do stuff like this for fun."

Daniel felt himself beaming at the idea of doing such things for fun. "It's pretty awesome," he said. He turned to Anna, who was smiling at him and blushing. She tucked some hair behind her ear. "I think *you're* pretty awesome," he added.

Anna reached out and grabbed his hand. Daniel felt chill bumps rush up and down his arms and legs. His scalp tingled, and his temperature rose.

"If I find out you have a girlfriend—" Anna began, heading off somewhere Daniel hadn't expected.

"I don't," he said quickly.

She took a step closer. "But if I find out you do, and this is some sorta post-hurricane game of yours, and the only reason you're hanging out with me is because I'm within walking distance and your girlfriend is stuck somewhere without a car—"

"I swear," Daniel said. He felt himself sweating from the surge of conflicting emotions, of arousal and fear.

"Because you see how creative I can get." She waved a hand at the pool. "My revenge would be ingenious."

"I've never really had a girlfriend in my li—"

Anna leaned forward and kissed him. It wasn't like his kiss with Amanda Hicks, forceful and raw and probing. It was soft and tender. Her lips seemed to jolt electricity into his, and he could feel the blood rushing out of his head, leaving him dizzy. Daniel didn't know what to do with his hands, but he wanted to do something special. He placed them on either of Anna's cheeks and held them there. Their lips remained pressed together, trembling.

When she pulled away, Daniel felt like crying for the loss, or maybe for the pure joy of it having happened. He was grinning like a fool, could feel his cheeks cramping. Anna smiled at him, her eyes fluttering, a look of pure contentment on her face.

"That was amazing," he whispered. He felt like such a fool for saying it. Like such a fool for starting his senior year and being so inexperienced with sex that a simple kiss could make him feel like he could fly. But he knew in that instant, as Anna nodded, silently agreeing with his assessment, that he was a *lucky* fool. For he had found a fellow reject, a girl too comfortable in her own skin to dress up and play like the others. He grabbed her hand and held it to his lips and kissed her fingers and fought the urge to say crazy things.

"Your dad is probably waiting on you," Anna said with a smile.

Daniel kissed her hand again. He knew if he wanted to, that he could bend forward and kiss her lips, her cheek, her nose, her forehead. The smile on her face said it was all possible. He was now a superhero elite. Nothing could stop him. His chest was cinderblocks full of glowing steel.

"I'll come see you tomorrow?" he asked.

"And the day after," Anna said.

Daniel smiled. As he ran down the steps, trying not to pass out and go tumbling head over heels, he found himself looking forward to a tomorrow for the first time in forever.

26

Daniel spent the night rolling around amid a tangle of blankets on Hunter's floor, his mind spinning as it dreamed of impossible things like being in love and moving massive trees off houses. The morning came with a clattering of chirping birds, their having returned from wherever the storm had blown them or wherever they had hidden away. Their songs roused Daniel from his first bit of good sleep; he woke and felt the summer's morning chill breezing through the window.

Daniel untangled himself, stood, stretched and looked out the window at the glowing and splintered forest beyond the back yard. Hunter lay on his back, his mouth wide open, the snuffles of contented sleep rattling in his throat.

"Lucky bastard," Daniel whispered. He walked quietly out the room and snuck into his own. His sister was lying on a bed made up of a sleeping bag and comforter, a single sheet draped over her from toes to shoulders. She turned her head away from the window and smiled at Daniel as he tip-toed toward his dresser. "Forgot to set out clothes," he whispered.

She nodded and turned to gaze at the brightening

sky. Daniel snuck a shirt and another pair of shorts out of his dresser, wondering when he was going to be able to wash what he'd worn the last few days. He stole a glance at his bed on the way out, which was mounded around his brother's girlfriend. One thing he and Hunter had agreed on while getting ready for bed the night before: their sleeping arrangements had been better off *before* they'd set out to "rescue" him.

Outside, Daniel felt the pleasing air of a Beaufort late-summer morning. There was a chill that the clear sky cautioned one to enjoy, for it would soon be burned off. The birds and squirrels were back to their foraging and mating games, giving the mortally wounded trees a film of life and activity. The waxy green of the leaves lucky enough to survive the storm glittered as the barest of breezes trembled through them. Everything seemed vibrant and sparkling and new. The day was awesome with possibility.

He carried a jug of water, two cups, and the last of the Pop-Tarts out toward the tool shed, finding that the spectacle of the day, or perhaps the kiss from the night before, had swept away a layer or two of resentment toward his father. The tool shed felt less and less apt a place for him. It had begun to seem cruel.

The front door of the shed was propped open to let in the nice air. His father was sitting on a bucket, tugging on his shoes. He looked up and smiled at Daniel, a few days growth on his face giving him a rugged appearance.

"Morning," he said.

"Morning, Dad." Daniel sniffed at the smell of gasoline. "You wanna eat out here?" Daniel looked to the yard. "There's plenty of logs to sit on."

His father laughed. "Sure. Same grub as yesterday?"

Daniel looked at the supplies in his hands. It looked like prison food. His dad stood and slapped him on the back. "I love Pop-Tarts," he said. "Boat food." He waved toward one of the bigger trees laying on its side in the yard.

"You been seeing this Anna girl for long?" his dad asked, sitting down. He looked up at Daniel as they both peeled back the metal foil and chewed on the cold and dry pastries. Daniel grabbed the cup from between his knees and took a sip.

"I met her the day after the storm," he said.

His father laughed. "I *thought* the thing between you two still had the shine on it."

Daniel felt a surge of anger at the mocking tone, dispelled at once by his father's pronouncement: "She seems like a great girl."

Daniel nodded and took another bite to keep his mouth busy with other things. He didn't feel like his dad had earned the right to know about his personal life.

"How in the world are we gonna get rid of *that* thing." He jabbed his Pop-Tart at the green plume of leaves sticking up over the roof. The tree seemed bigger than the house.

"A piece at a time," his father said. "That's how most things get done, good or bad. A piece at a time."

He took a long pull from his cup of water.

"I wish I could take some things back," his father said quietly. He looked off into the woods, and Daniel could feel his own eyes coat with tears. He lost himself in his second pastry.

"When I built this house, a part of me *knew* I could do it. I'd done just about every piece of building a house at some point or another, even though I never stayed on a job long enough to see it from beginning to end. I didn't really have that—what would you call it? Like an unbroken chain of events—"

"A continuum," Daniel said.

"Yeah. I just had all these jobs I drank myself on and off of, going where the money was then splitting once I had a fistful."

Daniel's father turned to him, his eyes under a blanket of water. "I had a problem before I met your mother," he admitted. "I kept it from her. Kept it from my parents when I was at school. Kept it from my teachers. Hell, I didn't even know it was a problem for the longest time. I knew other kids along the same lines, drinking all the time. The people I worked with on job sites seemed to be no different. You never know, when you're so used to hiding things, just how much everyone else is hiding as well. Your demons become their demons."

He stopped to take a bite. Daniel listened to the birds sing.

"When I met your mom, I wanted to build her the world. You should've seen how pretty she was." He shook his head and smiled. "So I talked myself and my future up, and I even believed some of it. That's what you do when you fall in love, or what most people do. They put this impossibly perfect thing up there for the other person to destroy, or figure out for a lie—"

"That's not how it has to be," Daniel said, even though he knew he had no idea about such things.

"I wish it wasn't," his father said. "With your kids, it's even harder. You guys looked up to me so much, right from the start. It was confusing. I already knew what a shit I was then, but you guys thought I knew everything—"

Daniel felt his body stiffen as his father lost it. His dad sobbed, his Pop-Tart in the dirt, his hands over his face. "And the bad gets built one piece at a time, too," he sputtered. "You don't know how it gets there, this thing you become, but looking back, it's like you drew it out with a pencil—"

"Dad—" Daniel whispered.

His father wiped his hands on his thighs and stared down at the dirt between his feet. Daniel saw tears plummet into the leaves and disappear in the dew.

"I never meant to be a bad father—"

"But you were," Daniel said.

"I know." His head bobbed. "I wish I could tell you what it's like to be old and full of regret. How you want to turn back the clock, how you pray for it every night, for one more giant chance to redo everything in your life. But even then, even knowing how those mistakes feel, you keep right on making them. You build and build on this awful foundation, you know? It's like you know there's a better way, but you can't start over. You want to do things different, but you keep right on like before. That's the curse of it all, Son. You learn what you're doing is wrong and bad, and you watch yourself spin in circles. You feel lost in the woods, but your footsteps are right there in front of you."

He sniffed and wiped his nose.

"I can't apologize for what I've put you kids through. There's no way I can make it up to your mom, and I'm not trying. When I leave the next time, as soon as I can, it'll be some short and foreign life I go off to try and live." His father looked at him, and Daniel realized he was crying as well. "I want you to know that you never have to forgive me, 'cause I'll never forgive myself."

"Dad—"

Daniel didn't know what to say.

"I just hope you'll do everything different than I did. You've got this chance ahead of you that I'd kill for. I'm so jealous and proud of you for that."

"Dad. I'm sorry for some of the things I said to you back then."

"I deserved worse."

"I'm still sorry. I wish I hadn't. I used to blame myself—"

"Oh God, Son." His father shook his head; his shoulders shook with sobs. "Son, please don't ever—"

"I don't anymore—"

"God, Son, don't ever blame yourself. I was a mess before I made you." He swiped the tears from his cheeks and wiped his nose. Daniel stood. He reached over and put his hand on his dad's shoulder, the most and least he could think to do, and his father's weathered hand came up to rest on it, holding it there. And his father cried even harder. His bent body was wracked by sobs, tears falling through the fingers of his other hand, which he kept over his face as if to hide from his son, or from the world. He cried and squeezed Daniel's fingers, pinning them to himself, and Daniel could tell what the simple gesture meant.

It made him wish he could offer or mean even more.

27

"Step through this loop first."

An hour later, faces dry, Daniel's father held a curl of webbing open at his feet. Daniel stepped through, shifted his weight to that foot, then did the same with the other.

"Now pull it up, just like a pair of shorts."

"This'll hold us if we fall?" Daniel shrugged the webbing up over his shorts, tugging down at the hem of them to keep them from getting bunched up.

"You could swing from this all day."

Zola watched them from the front steps, sucking on a straw punched through a warm juice box. Every now and then, she tried making a call or sending a text. Now, when she put her phone aside with each network error, it was with a practiced calm, none of the frustrated desperation from last night. Her straw slurped at the bottom of the box.

"You'd better be real careful with my boys up there," their mother said. She stood near one of the log piles, her arms crossed, a doubting look on her face. Daniel smiled at her to try and calm her nerves—and his. Carlton topped up the oil and gas on the chainsaw, then walked over and peered up the ladder leaning against the gutter. Hunter worked his homemade harness of knotted webbing on without their father's help.

"Knot your line on the other line like this when we get up there." He refreshed them on how to tie a bowline; the lessons taught on the houseboat years ago came flooding back, and the loss of the boat gnawed at Daniel. He untied and retied the knot several times while their father bent to secure a short piece of rope to the chainsaw. He stood, slung it over his shoulder, and went to the ladder first. The long, extended aluminum sides bent with his weight. He took the rungs slowly, getting both feet in place before reaching up with one hand to steady himself on a higher rung.

Once at the gutter, he lifted the chainsaw to a two-by-four he'd nailed in place across the shingles. He hoisted himself up and tied his webbing off to a loop of rope strung across the breadth of the house, from one side to the other. The loose bowline let him slide left and right and crawl higher up the roof, but should catch him if he slipped. Daniel watched, nerves tickling his stomach, as he waited for his dad to move out of the way. Then he went up the ladder after him.

The slope of the yard made the house feel more like three stories on that side, the unfinished basement letting out on the edge of the house around from where the tree hit. Daniel watched the bushes grow smaller as he went up. He reached the gutter and steadied himself while he tied the bowline. His dad watched while he made the twist, checking to make sure he did it in the right direction.

"Dear God, please be careful," his mother said.

"Don't take *forever*," Hunter offered. Chen and Zola

looked up from the limb they'd been dragging, shielding their eyes from the morning glare.

Daniel finished the knot and scrambled to the side, the edges of his sneakers clinging to the two-by-four. The ladder rattled as his brother started the climb up.

"Hold this in place," his father said. Daniel turned and grasped another two-by-four held against the roof. His dad extracted a hammer from his tool belt, shoved a few nails between his lips, and pressed one against the wood. A few expert strikes from his hammer, and one end of the board was fixed in place. He slammed another home, then passed the hammer and final nail to Daniel.

Daniel took his time pounding the nail in. His brother made it to the top of the ladder and worked on his knot.

"Up we go," their father said.

Daniel took another look down at all the gawkers looking back up. Carlton had started up the ladder, bringing them some more tools. Hunter followed their dad onto the next two-by-four, brushing up against one of the massive limbs bent across the shingles. Climbing up the roof was like ascending a man-made intrusion into a natural canopy. The leaves and boughs were in a tangle across the house that had seemed manageable from the ground. Now that he was up within it, Daniel saw the incredible task ahead of them.

"Here," Carlton said. He handed up the clippers and handsaw that had been kept busy over the last few days, chopping up anything small enough not to bother with the chainsaw. Daniel took the long-handled clippers and passed the saw to Hunter. The two of them moved to the first limb while their dad adjusted the loop of rope they were all attached to. Clipping the smaller limbs, they let the branches slide down toward the gutter, some of them getting caught up on the two-by-fours. They kicked these off, and Carlton helped remove them from the top of the ladder.

"You might want to get down and take the ladder with you," their father said. "Go around to the other side and we'll lower the first big one."

Carlton nodded and descended the ladder. Daniel and Hunter worked to clean the limbs on the way up, forging a path past their father and over the large boughs leaning against the house. Daniel still didn't see how the tree was going to be removed. He imagined a large crane would be necessary.

As they climbed, the limbs branching out overhead shaded them from the sun. Now they had truly ascended into a canopy. Daniel passed a fat limb that had snapped in half, the yellow and jagged interior revealing splinters the size of baseball bats. Their father climbed up beside them with a litheness that belied his age. He seemed to have become younger with the transition to a tilted, dangerous world, as if he had lived there much of his life.

"Stop at the peak," he told them.

Daniel and Hunter clung to a limb at the roof's apex. Their dad adjusted the rope holding the three of them to their tethered harnesses. He then uncoiled the rope around his chest and tied a series of loops and knots around the massive limb draped over the house. The other end of the rope was wrapped around the main trunk of the tree several times.

"Hold this," their father told them.

Hunter and Daniel obeyed. They were in their father's realm. What he said mattered, had force. This fact was as dizzying as the heights.

They each held the rope, which was wound twice around the great trunk, then tied tightly to the limb with complex knots. Daniel leaned back on the rope, testing it and finding security in the way it held him to the roof. Their father climbed up and straddled the peak of the roof. He brushed a small limb out of his way. Daniel looked back and could see his mom staring up at them. She had moved further into the yard to see them better through a hole in the canopy.

"The friction of the rope will do all the work," their father said. "Just hold tight." He looked to both of them. Daniel glanced over to Hunter to see a serious calm on his face. "You ready?"

Both boys nodded.

Their father set the chainsaw on his knee and flipped a lever. He yanked the handle and the machine roared to life. A haze of smoke billowed out, and the saw grumbled angrily as their dad revved the motor. He checked with the boys one more time, then pressed the chain into the massive broken limb clinging to their house.

He cut in stages, working his way down to the core of the limb from two angles. When the last bit went, the limb sagged down on the rope, stretching it, but not far. The chainsaw fell quiet.

"Now play it out," he told them.

Daniel let some slack into the rope, and his brother did the same. They had to flick the line to get it going, but then the limb slid down the steep incline of the roof, the scratch of bark loud on the rough shingles.

"That's good," their father said, peeking over the side. He guided their efforts, having them hold up when the tree reached the other gutter. He and Carlton talked back and forth, the rattle of the aluminum ladder heard on the other side. Following their father's commands, they lowered the huge limb down to the wooden deck out of sight and far below. The rope sang out as the limb went over the edge, its full weight hanging. The coil of line around the tree bit hard, but gobbled hungrily at any slack they fed it.

Carlton yelled something.

"She's down," their father relayed.

The slack fed into the rope stayed there.

The three of them rested on the roof, smiling at one another. Daniel looked around at the canopy with a new perspective. He saw each large limb as a discrete unit, as a task that could be tackled in fifteen or twenty minutes. Their father moved to the next one in the way, and Daniel could even see how large chunks of the main trunk could be removed, careful of course not to hit the shingles with the chainsaw.

They set to work, pausing after the next limb to accept a thermos of water hauled up at the end of a line. After a while, the labor became routine, and the spectators on the ground began working to clear the smaller limbs as they were cut away and rained down. Daniel took special pleasure when he saw Anna down in the front yard with Edward, the two of them stopping by to see the progress. By then, he was moving around the tree and roof with ease, handling the lines as surely as after a long weekend on the boat. He and Hunter worked as a team, his older brother becoming something of an equal in the labor. And together, with their father, and under the admiring gaze of a girl he surely loved—however fast it had happened—they worked to clear the house his dad had long ago built. They worked until the only thing that remained was the tall trunk, stripped clean and leaning into the crushed dormer and the stove-in roof.

****

It was late when the three of them finally undid their harnesses and came down the ladder, one by one. Their father was the last one off the roof, pausing to tie a serious tangle of knots around the belly of the old tree. He rattled down the ladder last, and then collapsed it and carried it out of the way.

"I appreciate the use of the Bronco," he told Edward, who had returned with Anna for the last of the procedure.

"Absolutely," he said, smiling through his beard.

Their father seized the line hanging from the tree and walked with it through the front yard to the cul-de-sac where the Bronco had been backed up between debris piles. He wrapped the line around the bumper, tied a loop in one side, then fed the other side through the loop. With a series of tugs, he yanked the line incredibly tight, taking the slack out, tying the Bronco off to the tilting tree. The top of the taut line just barely cleared the massive root ball sticking up from the ground, the circular pit of missing dirt sitting like a bowl beneath.

"Four wheel drive?" Edward asked.

Their father nodded. "And we'll ride, just to add more weight." He waved to the boys, then got in the passenger seat. Chen and Zola ran out and joined Hunter in the back seat. Daniel and Anna crawled through the open window and sat in the back, looking out at the tree and the taut line from bumper to bough.

"Easy at first," their dad said.

The Bronco lurched forward, the tires groaning against the pavement, and the rope whined in complaint. It stretched, and the knot made a crunching sound as it adjusted itself.

"Stay to the side," Daniel told Anna, suddenly fearful of the pent-up ferocity of the line. He imagined it parting and coming straight through the back of the car.

The Bronco growled forward another foot, and the line crackled. The car moved again, and Daniel saw a worried look on Carlton's face, standing at the side of the root ball. He seemed to be shaking his head as if nothing was happening.

The engine revved; one tire spun a little; Daniel could smell exhaust, could hear the rope grinding against itself. And then something gave. He reached across the fearful void between himself and Anna, both still leaning away from the power of the line stretching off the bumper, and fumbled for her hand. The Bronco surged forward. Slack flew into the line, like it had parted, but it was from the movement of the tree. The line went tight again. Carlton and his mom flinched away from the root ball, then turned to study it.

Hunter whooped. It was hard to see, looking right at it, but the tree was moving. The root ball was lowering back to the earth. Without the heavy limbs, and with most of its upper trunk removed, the much lighter tree was being pulled down by its roots and by the growling Bronco. It suddenly lurched off the house and settled toward the ground, tilting dangerously, but then guided by the rope as Edward drove across the cul-de-sac. It ended up back where it once stood, pointing at the sky, a sad husk of a tree without its limbs, the mound of earth clinging to its roots returning to the large divot it had left behind.

The rope finally went slack, and Carlton waved. Even their mother was smiling as she looked back at the house with its one busted eye. The other kids in the car were cheering and hollering, and Daniel joined in. He squeezed Anna, who didn't seem to mind that he was covered in bark and roof gravel and damp with sweat.

They all poured out of the car to go and look. Carlton and their mom steered them away from the tree, as if it still posed some unsteady threat. Daniel gasped at the sight of the gaping hole in the roof, the interior of the house visible and open to the sky above. It was a wound, sure, a nasty shiner, but at least the offending blow had finally been removed.

28

Things didn't go back to normal; they went back to the way they were. The power company showed up a day later apologizing for the delays, explaining the hundreds of thousands who had been without power across the Low Country. They estimated it would be another week, at least, before the neighborhood had power.

Cell phone service was restored soon after that visit. Zola said she could go without a hot shower for the rest of her life, if only those bars remained. She and her friends wrote books to each other, one little line at a time, detailing their adventures from Hurricane Anna and her aftermath.

Chen's parents got in touch almost immediately after service returned. They made their way down from Columbia with a list of supplies relayed by Daniel's mom. They also brought an incredible buffet of fast food with them, a welcomed luxury. Edward and Anna came over to enjoy the feast. Hunter left with Chen and her parents to help out at their house. It didn't seem like he was going far now that he was again a phone call away. Their mother cried anyway.

Six days after the storm, Carlton finally got in touch with the mechanics and was able to get his car back, giving the family enough mobility to pick up supplies. Power was restored a day later to the grocery store; several of the convenience stores reopened soon after. Daniel's mom spent many hours on the phone with State Farm, mostly on hold, as they tried to find a rental and figure out when an adjuster could come see the car. The agent explained that they were as busy as they'd ever been and that it could take some time. She didn't even mention the house to them.

Daniel spent the next week on the roof with his father. His dad had rounded up some materials and supplies from old contractors he had worked for; the lines at Lowe's and Home Depot were too outrageous to consider. Houses everywhere wore bandages of blue tarps and plywood. Chainsaws and generators could not be had at any price. There were rumors of gouging as entrepreneurs from out of state came through with trailers full of both, selling them for twice the retail price. News trucks roamed Beaufort looking for such tidbits, reporting from ground zero, the point of impact, *landfall*.

Daniel felt removed from and above it all. He was too busy learning how to peel back shingles; cut sheathing with a handsaw; scab in rafters, which often meant hammering at awkward angles. He learned how to measure and cut plywood to fit, how to frame out a dormer, how to lay tar paper and tack it in place with roofing nails. A few times a day, Anna would come over to gauge their progress from the ground. Daniel would beam down at her, rattling off the day's work or holding his arms in a ta-da pose. She would laugh and bring water up the ladder and smile at him with all the promises of more moonlight strolls through the neighborhood, holding hands and talking, enjoying the dead silence of the powerless world, laughing and kissing.

It was a momentous day when one of his father's friends came through with a brand new window. They were laying shingles down when he pulled up in his truck and called out jovial insults to Daniel's father, dropping his tailgate with a bang. It took a few shims to get the fit right, but the window went in with little effort. A handful of nails locked it in place. A piece of damaged siding salvaged off the back of the house was cut to cover the house wrap. The last of the shingles went on, and from the exterior, at least, the house was healed over.

On that last day, after Daniel had climbed down the ladder with a load of tools and supplies, his father had remained on the roof. Daniel looked up from the ground and saw him resting on one of the toe-boards, that two-by-four he had helped nail into place over a week ago. His father looked over the new dormer—a seamless copy of the original on the other side of the roof. He turned from it and gazed out over the yard, and Daniel didn't ask or intrude into his thoughts. He went off to wash his hands and track down the smells from the kitchen, leaving his father to contemplate broken homes and what it took to mend them.

The next day, their father found a ride to Columbia, where there was plenty of work patching roofs. Daniel knew there was plenty more work even closer by, but didn't challenge the decision. He figured his dad wanted to leave while he was still wanted—or needed, at least—rather than after he'd made things worse. Or possibly, it was getting too hard to take for him: being around the family he left, feeling a stranger in the house he'd built. Rather than wait at the cul-de-sac for his friend to arrive, he had gathered his meager belongings, said his goodbyes, and walked to the end of the neighborhood to wait. He was to the end of the driveway when Daniel realized he'd left the chainsaw behind.

Meanwhile, there remained a lot of work to be done on the inside of the house. The damage from the storm, like much damage, was more than skin deep. Zola's room was a wreck; they took plenty of pictures, cataloged the damage, and slowly went to work. Bags and piles of sheetrock, strips of carpet, and mourned possessions went out. New insulation went in, covered by scraps of sheetrock it took half a day at Lowe's to secure. After mudding and painting, putting down more carpet, moving Hunter's bed into Zola's room, it almost looked like a room again, like someone could live there.

And then there was Anna.

It was unusual for a first named storm to form so late in the season, even more unusual for it to become such a perfect storm and do such damage. Nobody could remember an "A" storm having such an impact. All the same could be said of Daniel's Anna. From four houses down, she had come out of nowhere. She was as electronically unpopular as he, and Daniel found in their long walks and talks the sort of company he had been hunting for in the digital wilderness. In the two weeks he was out of school, and the neighborhood was without power, they hardly moved beyond holding hands, kissing, and lingering embraces. For Daniel, it was an inconceivable enough. He had gone from emotionally and romantically stunted to just right.

As he returned to school, and Anna continued her studies at home, Daniel found that he was moving into the world as an adult, despite his virginity. That last was now something he treasured and savored, rather than something he meant to destroy and conquer. He moved into the world as an adult with a secret, a man with a silly love in his heart, a girlfriend down the street that hardly any of his friends knew—and Daniel figured it was their loss.

****

"Dude!"

Roby waved from across the courtyard, a goofy grin on his face. Daniel dug his thumbs into the straps of his backpack and hurried over to meet him.

"I've been trying to call you for two days, man." Roby threw his arms around Daniel and slapped his backpack.

"I've had my phone off," Daniel said.

"What for?"

Daniel shrugged. "I got kinda used to not being reached at any time by whoever," he said. He left out that the "whoever" was usually his mom trying to get him to come home from Anna's house. "How've you been? Did you guys get much damage?"

Roby rolled his eyes. "Did we get much damage? Dude, we had half our windows blown in. Someone said the gusts got over one-sixty up on the hill behind us. We were in the eye wall for like an hour." He nodded his head. "What about you guys?"

Daniel shrugged. "Lots of trees down. One big one into the house. But it wasn't that bad."

"Sounds like you got lucky, then."

"I don't know about that," Daniel said.

"Hell yeah you did. Didn't you hear about Jeremy's house?"

"Jeremy Stevens?"

"Yeah, dumbass." Roby's eyes widened. "You remember the party, right? The night of the storm?"

"I guess," Daniel said. Some of that night drifted back to him. He remembered a ride in a cop car, loud music, having a little to drink—

"That's weird. I'd kinda already had forgotten about that." He scratched his head. "Probably because of all that came after. I mean, I had the worst two nights of sleep—"

"But you remember the video, don't you?" Roby narrowed his eyes. "Dude, it's all anyone's been talking about."

Daniel stared at him.

"The video of you and Amanda Hicks? Full frontal nudity? What the fuck, man?"

"Oh shit," Daniel said. "Oh fuck. Fuck me, dude." Sudden images of Anna sitting in front of her dad's computer, two hands over her mouth, Daniel spinning naked before her. "I'm totally screwed," Daniel said.

Roby laughed. "You have no idea how lucky you are, you shit! That video is like urban legend now. If you were one of the fifty or so people to see it, you're like in this cult."

"What do you mean?" Daniel was pretty sure he was going to throw up on the pavement. He felt like everyone walking past was looking right at him, smiling.

"Jeremy's house had flood damage. His home computer is toast."

"You're shittin' me." Daniel still felt sick. It was going to take days to pass. "But everyone's okay, right?"

Roby waved his hand. "Like that's more important. But yeah, it wasn't even from the storm, not directly. Their pool burst open and flooded half the downstairs."

Daniel clutched his shirt. "And the computer?"

"I tried everything." Roby frowned. "Couldn't save your little video."

"What do you mean? You went over there and tried to *salvage* it?"

"Like I want to see your little prick." Roby glanced around the courtyard. "I told Jeremy I would try and get their family stuff off the drive, pictures and documents and what-not, which I did."

"You did."

"Yeah. I plugged the drive into my computer. Worked like a charm. The motherboard was the only thing that got wet."

Daniel was about to explode. "For fuck's sakes, Roby, what the hell did you do?"

Roby smiled. "I put you in my debt for let's see . . . like, forever."

"You deleted it."

He raised his eyebrows and grinned coyly. "Or I kept a copy. You'll never know."

"Dude—"

"Speaking of which, we still have a ton of debris to round up and get rid of. I told mom that you'd be coming over this week and helping me do my share."

"Seriously, man? You're gonna blackmail me?"

His friend smiled. "Nothing I do to you will be worse than what I prevented."

"But you're my friend!"

"Yeah, well, then you should've gotten in touch with me at some point the past two weeks."

"Man, I'm sorry, I've been busy. And hey, it's not like we don't go all summer without hearing from each other—"

"Yeah, but this was like the storm of the *century*. I was dying to talk to you about everything that was going on."

Roby frowned. "I tried to get my mom to drive us by last week and see how you guys were doing, but my dad is still militant about the gas. We've been driving everywhere at like twenty miles an hour. I thought he was gonna cut a hole in the floor and go Flintstone on us."

Daniel laughed.

"I'm serious, dude. He got all end-of-the-world. You shoulda seen him. We were on rations for the first week."

The more grave Roby tried to look, the harder Daniel laughed.

"I'm glad you think my suffering is funny."

"Ditto. But hey, at least you got to spend a ton of time with your girlfriend, though, right?"

"I wish. She has an aunt and uncle nearby. She went to their house after the party and stayed there for the storm. I just saw her a week ago as she was heading back to Columbia. I think she's gonna come back down in a few weeks, if her parents and NOAA say it's alright."

Daniel laughed.

"I'm not kidding," he said. "Her parents have already set up hurricane rules for our weekends together."

"Guess what?" Daniel asked. He figured now was a good time to fully explain neglecting his friend the past weeks. "I kinda met someone after the storm."

"Yeah?" Roby's eyes lit up. "A girl?"

"Guess what her name is. I'll give you a hint: It's real ironic."

"Like *real* ironic or Alanis Morissette ironic?"

Daniel thought about that. "I'm not sure, actually."

"Her name's Wendy," Roby guessed.

Daniel laughed. "No, but close." He shrugged his bag higher up his back. "Her name's Anna."

Roby stopped laughing. "Serious?"

"Yeah, and we're like boyfriend and girlfriend."

"Who's playing the girlfriend?"

"Shut up, dude." The bell rang, signifying two minutes to class. Kids stood and stretched in the courtyard. Some hurried off, backpacks jouncing dangerously.

"What's this girl like?" Roby jerked his head to the side. "Walk while you tell me about her. And don't forget to kiss my ass for making sure the first time she sees you in the buff is the first time she sees you in the buff."

"No, honestly, thanks for that. You being Jeremy's geek-on-call worked out for me."

"The girl," Roby said, waving his hand in circles.

"Anna," Daniel replied. "This girl's a category five, to be sure. Insanely smart. Pretty in a normal kind of way, not like cheerleader pretty or tall and exotic—"

"Kinda plain?" Roby asked.

Daniel shook his head. "There's nothing plain about her."

Roby held open the door to the English building, and Daniel stepped inside and let his eyes adjust to the fluorescent lights. He wondered what he could say about Anna that wouldn't sound silly, wondered if maybe Roby felt the same way about his girlfriend, how much more he and his best friend might now have in common. But before he could think of the first thing to say, they passed a bulletin board with a weeks-old newspaper tacked up for the students to see.

"Holy shit," Daniel said. He stopped and stared at the full-page image on the cover of the Journal.

"You haven't seen this picture?" Roby asked.

Daniel shook his head. "Haven't really seen the news at all."

"Listen, I've got to run to the end of the hall. I'll catch up with you at lunch, okay? I want to hear about this girlfriend of yours."

Daniel nodded and waved him off.

"And I want my ass kissed properly," Roby yelled back as he blended in with the river of kids jostling and chattering down the hall.

Daniel barely heard him. He stood and stared at the newspaper behind the glass. In bold type across the top, it simply said: "ANNA STRIKES." Below that, and taking up the entire rest of the page, was a satellite photo. It showed a storm spread wide across the entire state of South Carolina, long trails of feeder bands curling down through the Atlantic, the northwest corner of the storm brushing Charlotte. But the part Daniel found himself transfixed on was the eye. There was a perfect circle in the center of the storm, a hole in the white shroud directly over Beaufort. Daniel stared through the glass display at the center of that hole and imagined himself down there, looking up at the blue sky, asking Carlton if the worst was over. And Carlton was saying it had just begun.

It felt like a lifetime ago. Like something a different person had lived through. Daniel lost himself in that image and the memory of a temporary quiet at the center of so much noise and destruction, and he realized, in an instant, that the *eye* was the storm. That low pressure at the middle, that intense calm and quietude surrounded by a wall of maelstrom, *that* was the hurricane. It's power came from the sucking void, was shaped by the spinning of the world, was fed by the warmth of the seas, and it had churned quietly along, oblivious and uncaring, passing right over his home, whipping an unknown frenzy across his life with its wide and powerful winds, rocking him, changing him, with its mighty calm.

This book is dedicated to those who lost
their lives or loved ones during the
horrific storm season of 2011.

Made in the USA
Middletown, DE
01 April 2022

63507941R00135